MW01113715

ONE LAST CHANCE

FOUR BEST FRIENDS

Kaleem'Abdul'Adl

Pensive Writers LLC.
CEO Jonathan Bernard
Kaleemabduladl@yahoo.com
facebook.com/kaleemabduladl

ISBN-13: 978-1533137128
ISBN-10: 1533137129

Printed in the USA

Edited by: Lotus Blossom Creations
lotusblossomcreative.net
lotusblossomcreative@gmail.com

Kaleem 'Abdul 'Adl

DEDICATION

I dedicate the good that comes out of this book to my children, from the youngest to the oldest.

Jayla - Do you remember when you were a baby and you used to try to pull my beard out, lol. I'm so sorry I missed your childhood years. It will never be too late for us to unite. You will always be my Baby, little girl; and I will always be your Father and be there for you. I love you.

Ja'Myah - There's nothing I can imagine that could ever touch my heart more than you making Salah (prayer) with me when I was out, unless and except you take your shahadataiyn. No distance or time away from you could ever sever my love for you. You will always be my Pretty Little Princess, and I will give you the shirt off my back if that was all I had. I love you.

Jon'nae - My darling little girl is a young lady now. You may not remember but I remember you falling asleep on my chest, so you're always going to be my Darling Little Girl. You've grown into a beautiful young lady. Always put Allah first and worship Him alone, without any partners. I love you.

Ja'Quante - My only son and my eldest. My love for you may seem tough because it's the best love to make you a man. You have sisters to look over in my absence so no knucklehead man will take advantage of them. I know you won't let me down, and I believe in you. Never give up and always strive to be the best at whatever you do. I love you.

May Allah guide all of you to the Musta Qeem (straight path).

ACKNOWLEDGMENT I

One thing for sure is that I acknowledge that there is no deity worthy of being worshiped in truth except Allah Ta'Ala (God Most High) and that Muhammad ibn 'Abdullah, peace and blessings be upon him, is His servant-slave Messenger.

I acknowledge my shortcomings and strive to follow the truth and not my desire and hope that Allah will have mercy on me. Because without His Ta'Ala's (The Most High) mercy, we will all be doomed.

All of what is bad and evil in this book is from my evil desires that I fight every day not to act upon, and the Shaytan (Satan).

Whatever is good and guidance in this book is from the ONE above the heavens and earth. I hope that people will benefit from both the good and evil. The good by those who try to act upon it, and the bad by people learning about it, to avoid it, hoping the readers will refrain from it.

ACKNOWLEDGEMENT II

I appreciate everything you all have done for me in your contributions to the success of this book.

Taiasha - You are my baby sister. Hold on until big bro comes home. I promise I got you. I appreciate your contribution in helping me publish my book.

Tyrone - My baby brother. I'm proud of you. You're next with your comic book. I believe in you.

Kejo - I admire your dedication and hard work you do for your wife and kids.

Gina - I really appreciate you helping me with my book. I never told you, but before I got locked up, you became my favorite Auntie.

Billionaire Book Bros. - From the bottom we are, to the top we go. Keep banging the industry up with them fire hot books.

Trap House Publication 386 - I appreciate the time and knowledge you all shared about the writing industry with me. Keep moving forward and don't ever quit. I'll meet yall at the top!

Vernon - I've known you since elementary school, and we've been friends from then up to this day, and you're still in my corner. You are the epitome of a true friend.

Jamal - Love you solely for the sake of Allah. Since the day we met, I vibed with you. I appreciate everything you do for me on the West Coast.

<u>C-Wakely</u> – Real recognize real. Appreciate everything bro. We going to keep it moving no matter what. Big things for real men coming soon. We'll be there!!!!!

<u>White Boi Pizzal</u> - You shocked me with your support. I'm glad you're on my team. We're taking over when I come home.

<u>B.</u> - We met on a business adventure and clicked like we were childhood friends. We're going to the top! Just hold on!

<u>Untamed</u> - Keep your head up! It ain't over. I have faith in you.

<u>Jugga James</u> - You've been riding with me since the beginning of the Killa Gorillas, and you're still here. I'm glad to have you as a friend and one on my team. May Allah guide you.

<u>James Mcfadyen</u> "The White Wonder" - I appreciate you for making things easier for me. The more you learn about the urban culture, the better you're becoming at working in this genre. You've done a great job!

<u>Frank Wallace</u> - I give it up to ya bra. Hold it down in South Carolina. Thanks for all your input.

ACKNOWLEDGEMENT III

One time for all of those who never turned their back in my time of absence.

Suzzy - You will always be my Sugar Plum. I love you girl. Please forgive me. All the wrong I have done to you and you never turned your back on me. If I had a chance to do it all over again, I would have married you. May Allah guide you to the truth.

Jessica - What's up Cuz? Keep being that strong Black Beautiful Queen that you are. I'm proud of you.

Tawana and your husband Jonathan - I am so proud to have you as the Mother of my children, and I thank you for everything you have done for me. You married a good respectable man which means that's good for my children. I thank Allah for having the both of you supporting me throughout my absence and raising my children. I appreciate you Jonathan for your support and understanding.

Ismaeel - As Salaamu 'Alaikum wa rahma tullahi wa barakatuhu. As long as we got Allah and He guides us to the Mustaqeem, that's worth more than anything in the world. I love you solely for the sake of Allah.

Torray - As Salaamu 'Alaikum. I love you solely for the sake of Allah. You've always kept it real with me and had my back. I'll never forget that. I'm so glad that you're my brother in faith.

Hamp - As Salaamu 'Alaikum. I love you solely for the sake of

Allah. When I was young and didn't have anybody, you were there. You fought off the bullies before I came out the box. I'm out now! And I will always fight for you.

Big Rico - We both were under pressure together and neither one of us bust. I respect you for that. I also appreciate everything you've done for me while I'm at my lowest.

Corey - Keep your head up bro. Inshaa Allah (God Willing) you'll give it back. We're going to make the best with what we've got.

Pimp Shawn - It ain't over bro. We're going to make it out of this, so tell them haters to kick rocks. I pray that Allah guides you to be my brother in faith (Islam).

9MM POP - One of my favorite artists who makes me laugh. If we had recorded our times together as the Killa Gorillas, we woulda had the number one reality show. Keep your head up bro.

Tony (A.P.K.) - I love you solely for the sake of Allah. I'll never forget that personal letter you wrote me when we were in the County together. It meant a lot to me and I still have the letter.

Michael Lester (Slim) - A real soldier and true friend forever who kept it real. I'm proud of you bro.

Kareem - A.P.K. representer. The realist from that City. When the pressure came, you didn't bust like all them other police-ass niggas. No matter what, I'ma always have your back and I love you for that.

Paula Fair - Your letter meant a lot to me. It let me know you didn't forget about me. I got ya when I come home! Love ya!

Khadafee AKA Flee – Ft. Lauderdale representer. As Salaamu 'Alaikum. You were always special to me. I can't wait until we kick it and bump our heads together on the other side. I love you solely for the sake of Allah.

<u>Hilal Tariq</u> - As Salaamu 'Alaikum. I appreciate everything you have done for the Muslims here at Coleman Community. You went home and kept it real. You sent back books, letters, and money to more than one Muslim. I love you solely for the sake of Allah. May Allah keep you safe and aid you in this crazy dunya.

<u>Zakee</u> - As Salaamu 'Alaikum. My favorite Muslim. I love you solely for the sake of Allah. I miss ya bra. I'll be up there to Savannah to see ya.

<u>All of my Salafee Muslim brothers</u> - who I didn't mention, I did so out of respect for you. I love all of you for the sake of Allah. I pray for you all and please pray for Allah to guide me to that which is better. No matter what, Inshaa'Allah, my salaat will never cease, major shirk I will never commit and sins I try to repent and strive not to repeat.

A SPECIAL DEDICATION
TO MY PARENTS WHO RAISED ME

Mrs. Bernard - Mom, I'm sorry for all the pain I took you through. Please forgive me. I understand now because of what Islam has taught me BY HIS WILL. I appreciate your tough love and I got you when I come home. I love you.

Lay - You loved me in a special way that I will never be able to get from anyone else. You were the only man I accepted after my biological father. I ran them other niggas off from my mom. You taught me how to love another man's child, and I appreciate you for that. I thank you for being my stepfather, and I got you too when I come home. I love you.

No - My biological father. Allah says to never sever the ties of kinship. Allah chose you to produce me, and my two brothers and sister BY HIS WILL. And I recognize you for that. We had fun in the streets and on the block together, but Islam has taught me that all fun ain't good fun. But on another note, I love you and hope that you become clean.

PROLOGUE

One Last Chance is a series of books that separate themselves from the more common urban genre of books. Among the distinguishing features of the One Last Chance series is a voice, a second narrative voice that brings an awareness due to the consequences of the characters in the book when they make bad decisions, which would enlighten the reader's conscience as to the foolhardy things we do for stupid reasons. One Last Chance will show you wisdom from different aspects of life.

As you read the books, you will be able to compare street knowledge to religious knowledge, learning that the latter is the best guidance for one's life. By reading these books, anyone not from the streets will be able to learn and acquire an understanding as to why many Black men and women do the things we do that keeps us in poverty. Many of us then try to get out of poverty by doing illegal things that land us in prison, away from our families.

Conversely, by reading these books, anyone from the streets will be able to learn about the other world, the legitimate world, given an insight from a different perspective and a better way of living life.

Book I of One Last Chance journeys throughout the lives of four childhood friends from Orlando, Florida who meet again as teenagers, and want more than what they ask for, thinking the dope game is the key to the answer.

KINO has the brains, yet like so many others, he falls short due to his desire and lack of positive role models. MURK has the heart and muscle, but uses them without thinking or caring about the end result. All COUPE want to do is floss; he will do anything to keep his flossing status like his father, Pastor Placky. POOCHY just follows along and fits in, trying to help his Mother, little sister, and Grandfather.

Through their excursions, the reader will be able to reflect on their own life and learn to take admonition from the wrong choices of these characters, to the betterment of one's self.

Will they succeed and become one of the few who will make it out of the streets, without regretting and wishing they had **ONE LAST CHANCE?**

There's a difference between
• Telling and teaching
• When to speak and when not to speak
• When to fight and when to walk away
Learn the difference between them, and your life will become better.

-Kaleem 'Abdul 'Adl-

CHAPTER ONE

Kino was born in Philadelphia to Dorothy and Derick Betterman. They live in Willingboro, New Jersey. Kino's father left for Florida to get away from the fast street life of Camden and Philly only to find himself right back in the game.

Same thing, same streets, same direction, just a different place in a different lane, the course and end results Derick Betterman was heading for did not change, because he was doing the SAME THING.

Kino was one-year-old when his father was arrested on one count of first-degree murder, and one count of attempted murder. Leaving Kino and his mother alone to fight poverty and plight, resulting from living in a disoriented broken home in the ghetto, with no man in the house.

The man is the eternal, undisputed leader, ordained by Allah, with the ability to lead his family. Metaphorically, the family is the body, and of that body, the Father is the head and the Mother is the heart. The head leads with intellect and the heart leads with emotions. Once the head (i.e. the Father) is removed, then the family is led by emotions (i.e. the Mother) and women are emotional creatures.

It's 1:20 p.m., he is sitting on a hard concrete block, cold as the North Pole, waiting anxiously to hear from his public pretender. Today, D-Bo's day began at 4:00 a.m. when they woke him up and moved him to the transporting cell of the Orange County Jail in Orlando, Florida. It's been three hours in that ice box of confinement. A colorless scenery, white concrete block walls, concrete bench seats painted with a primer gray color. Metal toilet, metal sink. Rusted bars for a gate, painted white. Dirty and dingy looking with names written and carved on the wall, "so and so been here." No covers, no pillows except for a toilet roll being used as one.

Being transported to the courthouse, it's now 7:00 a.m. and this chamber under the courthouse building is no warmer in color or temperature than the cell he just left. The best thing so far for him was the ten-minute ride through the city. He will be in this confinement for another six hours, just staring at three walls and bars, giving him plenty of time to contemplate the omens running through his mind that lead up to this day. D-Bo is facing natural life without parole if he loses at trial. His plea bargain is for twenty-five years. Thinking to himself, "*twenty-five years, that might as well be life.*"

Sitting with his two elbows on his knees, hands holding his face looking down to the ground, the Correctional Officer called his name, "Derick Betterman, attorney interview." His heart beating with every step he took, waiting to exhale a breath of relief as he sat down to speak to the public pretender.

"Here's the deal. They have their witnesses and they're ready to go to trial."

"*I can't believe they came to court,*" D-Bo said to himself without thinking who or which of the witnesses were present. It never crossed his mind to ask the public pretender if the main witnesses were showing up because he had a million things running through his head at one time. The public pretender deceived D-Bo, presenting the situation as if the main witnesses were showing up for trial. As D-Bo's brain started to clear up from the fog of undesirable thoughts of him doing life in prison, because some punks who robbed him caused D-Bo to retaliate on them. He thought, "Now they want to come to court like some punk ass niggas."

Black-on-Black crime becomes Black-on-Black genocide. Either death or life in prison is what we are doing to one another.

Before D-Bo could get a word out of his mouth...

"Look, I got them to come off the twenty-five years. Twenty is on the table, but I might be able to get them down to fifteen, running concurrent," the public pretender said.

D-Bo sat back to think. "If them bastards wasn't coming to court, I would be going home today to my child and lady. Twenty years is better than twenty-five years, and a whole lot better than natural life, if I lose at trial." Then he thought some more. "Hell no. Twenty years is still a long time." He paces back and forth, bewildered about what to do. One hour later the public pretender comes back.

"Look, I got them down to fifteen years, followed by ten years' probation. You have two and a half years in. Doing eighty-five percent, you could be home around ten to eleven years from now with your son and wife. WE can take a risk and go to trial but, if WE lose, YOU would be looking at natural life, without parole."

Notice how the public pretender emphasizes we until it comes to doing the time, then he emphasizes you?

D-Bo is frustrated in pain as anxiety runs through his heart, feeling like he should not be in this predicament in the first place. D-Bo was the one who got robbed, with the impression that he is the victim. The person he killed and the one he shot deserved what came to them, for tying up his mother and then raping his wife. The other two punks who aided and abetted them want to come to court and testify against D-Bo because D-Bo tried to kill them too, but his bullets missed them, he ran out of lead and they got away.

D-Bo sat down to reminisce on him holding his baby boy Kino when he was newborn, and as a baby. Now that Kino is running, jumping, talking and walking, it will be another eleven years before D-Bo could interact with him in the free society, if he pleas out. On the contrary, if he goes to trial and loses, he receives natural life without parole. D-Bo thought he would be feeling the insides of his wife today, he just knew he was going home. Allah had a different plan.

These cats want to live the street life, but don't want to abide by the street codes and rules. If you can't do the time, don't do the crime, what goes around comes around, so when it comes back on you take it like a man. Know that it might not come back the same time or in the same way, but know that it's coming back.

So don't dish out what you don't want to come back to you. Tying up someone's Mother alone is enough to sign your death warrant, let alone raping his wife too. If the streets were the jury, the verdict would be: "Free D-Bo!"

"I'm already doing two life sentences and all you can do is reduce one life sentence to fifteen years, but I'm still stuck with the other life sentence," said the prosecutor's main witness.

"Derick did shoot you three times and killed your best friend, right?" the prosecutor asked, trying to persuade his must-needed witness to win this case.

"If you can't get both of my life sentences dropped then I don't know who shot me nor who killed my friend." Some type of light clicked on in his head while he was listening to the prosecutor feeding him bull crap.

He was feeling bad for what they did to D-Bo and his family. Realizing the Black-on-Black crime and the Black-on-Black snitching, sending each other to jail by cooperating with the law enforcement. They don't want justice. They want just-us behind bars. The government wants a conviction, Black or White. It just so happens that Blacks are helping them get their convictions for the wrong reasons. Doing it to get time off your sentence or for a vindictive motive is not the morally street way of life. If you think there's no such thing as street morals, then ask Tony Montana why he shot that hitman from Panama in the head when they were in the car.

"Go suck a turtle's cock, and give me more time to add to my two life sentences if you want to. I ain't testifying." This is the reason the prosecutor backed off the twenty-five years and offered Derick fifteen years.

His public pretender knew what was going on because he and the prosecutor made a deal to trade Derick's conviction for another person's freedom. The person to be freed would receive time served for his conviction. The other witnesses who D-Bo shot at were nowhere to be found, fearing for their lives, and the police with criminal charges. The other witnesses that the prosecutor had could not identify D-Bo as the shooter. Little did D-Bo know that he could walk free if he stands in the paint and goes to trial.

"Let's get this over with. I'll take the fifteen years. My son will be fourteen, I can catch his teenage years."
"I knew you were smart. I didn't want all that good negotiation and begging I did to get you down to fifteen years to go to waste," the public pretender said, as he patted Derick on the back as if he were doing Derick a favor.

CHAPTER TWO

Kino went to six different elementary schools, growing up in Orlando, Florida. His Mother was unstable, being evicted from several apartments, moving from friends to family members. This roller coaster ride affected Kino's ability to be in a comfort zone. After adjusting to newly met friends and teachers, he would be forced to pack it up and move again. Always starting over for Kino became a part of his life at an early age.

It was at Ivey Lane Elementary School where he met his three compadres - Murk, Poochy, and Coupe. Murk's parents were drug addicts. By the time he reached Middle School, Murk had experienced and witnessed more than the average adult.

The downside to this is that he learned and experienced what the streets offered while neglecting his education. Have you ever seen a thug who can't fill out an application? Well, Murk is your answer. Do we as Black people understand that home is where it starts and a child being raised in a hostile drug-infested environment with survival worries on his mind makes it hard for him or her to go to school and learn? So they act out by disturbing class. A Caucasian teacher does not understand their situation and becomes scared then sends the students to the office. As they grow older, it is no longer the teacher but now the police. Just like the teacher sent the students to the office, the police send them to jail. As far as the Black teachers, they are either Uncle Tom bourgeois want-to-be upper-class people or ones who have twenty-something students and doesn't have the time to attend this individual child. This child needs special counseling and teachers. The end result is, the teacher passes them through school or he drops out, or is sent away to Juvenile Detention Centers. They also often end up receiving no education, becoming a thug who can't fill out an application for a job.

Murk ended up stabbing his step-father and got waived over as an adult and sentenced to prison. Most of his incarceration he stayed in confinement. Just like school, he kept getting into trouble with the officers and fights with the inmates. He never got his G.E.D. The six grade was the highest level he completed, even though he got passed through as he cheated on the FCAT Test. Due to his incarceration, he became institutionalized at an early age.

Murk's mother died of an overdose of heroin in his second year of incarceration. Her husband, who Murk stabbed, hoodwinked Murk's Mother, introducing her the drug as a new kind of cocaine.

Murk's biological father is serving a life sentence. His Mother was the only person who sent him money when she was able, the only person who wrote him, who came to visit him. She died when he was only fourteen years old. Once she left his life, the system became his family, showing him no love, only making him stock. He fell into the trap of becoming stock, a returning cycle in and out of jail to fuel the fire of a billion-dollar industry filling up the penitentiaries.

Why don't Afro-Americans realize that this is a form of modern-day slavery? We are falling for it. The system is not built to correct you, but to institutionalize you. So they can make an income off you. Nobody to prosecute, nobody to fill the jails. No jobs for the people. The ruse is aimed at the tax payer's mind to justify the amount of monetary dividends allocated to fight crime. Even when the economy is doing bad, the government employees manage to get pay raises, paid vacations, bonuses, with the best benefits of health and life insurance, not to mention their pensions. All paid for by the tax payer's dollar. So wake up and smell the coffee. We live in a capitalistic society. It is sad that the majority of Black men decide to become stock as opposed to pursuing a professional status of a doctor, lawyer, or becoming a business mogul, or a slave to Allah, which is the best. Certain people do not want you competing with them to become lawyers, doctors, President of the United States, or any professional job. So they find a way to subliminally trick you, keeping you right where they want you to be --- Locked Up ---. Of course, they don't force you. It is a choice we make. So let's start making better choices.

Kino's friend Poochy was raised in a religious home. His family was in the church heavy. His parents were deep rooted sanctified Christians. His Mother would catch (what some people call) the Holy Ghost every Sunday and speak in tongues. His Grandfather was the preacher. They didn't have a big church, it was more of a family church, right in the middle of the ghetto of APK Apopka, Florida.

Their family didn't take people for their money, nor did they ask for money. It was the church of real. They tried to be real with God. They were also extremely poor. Poverty was their followers, their environment, and the church's middle name. The congregation ranged from crackheads to alcoholics to transients and the lower class poor people. When it was time for offering, the church could not collect half of the money for rent.

Now Coupe, on the other hand, his parents were preachers who owned their church, which catered to Black doctors, lawyers and the bourgeois class of people. Coupe's Father name was Pastor Placky. Some called him Pastor Pimp, cause he sure was pimpin' his churchgoers all the way to the bank. They say the apple don't fall far from the tree so you can imagine what Coupe was like.

When they (Kino, Murk, Poochy, and Coupe) were growing up, Coupe was always in competition with Kino. He had to be number one and no one could out do him. All of the girls liked Kino despite Coupe's flamboyant style. So a rage of envy always kindled inside of Coupe against Kino.

Murk was eighteen years old when he was released from prison. His crew, Kino, Poochy, and Coupe, were in the twelfth grade. With his Father serving life and his mother dead, Mrs. B., Kino's mother, took Murk in with open arms. She had been friends with Murk's Mother.

Being on probation, he was counseled to enroll in a G.E.D. program and get a job. Kino and his Mother stayed in Peppertree Apartments, across the street from the Palms Apartments on Mercy Drive, where everybody and their mammy was selling crack. Even the kids in middle school were selling crack.

Kino and his click went job searching. McDonald's decided to give them a chance, except for Murk. He was too ashamed to ask for help filling out the application. When the Manager saw misspelled words, a lot of blank spaces, sloppy handwriting with no experience, no education, he became skeptical about hiring Murk. So he ran a background check.

"Attempted Murder?   Hell no!" the Manager said to himself when the record came back. This was basically the same story everywhere Murk went to try to get a job.

Pastor Placky got one of his friends to hire Coupe as a salesman in a furniture store.

When Kino got paid he had to help his Mother with the bills and Poochy was trying to help his Grandfather, whom he loved dearly, from having the church foreclosed. Murk was mad at the world; no mother, no father, no education, and no job. Getting turned down every which way he went. One day, Murk slept in and Mrs. Betterman was on the speaker phone while getting dressed for work.

"Please just give me one more week to pay you. If you

repossess my car, I will not be able to get to work and school. After this semester, I will be looking for a part time job to help me catch up with the back-pay that I owe you."

"Well, if you like, we can discuss this over dinner about other ways you can pay for it if you know what I mean," he said in a seductive voice.

"I will have your damn money, cause I'm not no whore!" Then she hung up on him and started crying.

Before you know it, a tear dropped out of Murk's eye, feeling sympathy for Mrs. B., causing him to think about his twin sister, who his Step-father molested.

CHAPTER THREE

Kino missed the bus because the teacher put him on detention for something he didn't do. By the time he got to work, he had got written up and was told that if he's late again, he will get fired.

"Kino, what happened?" Poochy asked.

"Mr. Rianhart thought I was talking when it was Coupe, and you know I ain't no snitch, so he put me on after-school detention."

"Man, that's messed up. Why Coupe didn't speak up and claim the fame like he always do?"

"I don't know bro. "

"I tried to hold the bus, after a while you already know the deal."

Kino gave Poochy some dap and told him, "I appreciate you, bro."

"Yall going to the club Sunday?" a co-worker asked them.

"I don't know, I have to clean Sunday, plus I promised to give half of my check to Grandpop for the church and the other half to my Mom for rent," said Poochy

"I'm supposed to give my whole check to my Mom to help pay rent." Kino pauses and thinks, "Rent's not even due for another two weeks. "

"Umm, excuse me, are you gossiping or working?" asked a customer.

She was five feet, six inches tall and weighed a hundred and thirty-five pounds, with big brown eyes, warming pretty smile, and beautiful pecan tan smooth skin. Her breasts were the size of tennis balls that stood up. She had long silky Indian jet-black natural straight hair. Her big, round, soft ass had a little jiggle, but not too much. Her hourglass body shape was cute as hell, and she had a soft, not loud, intelligent ghetto voice.

Kino was stuck in a daze, mouth wide open with his bottom jaw about to fall off his face, his tongue hanging out like a dog panting in the heat.

"Kino!" yells Poochy. "Take the girl's order."

"Yes, may I help you?"

"Let me get a hamburger kids meal."

"Will that be it?" Kino asks.

"Can I ride on the slide?" a little girl came running up.

"Go back over there by Khadeeja until I come over there. Yall are going to split this food, then you can play for fifteen minutes because we have to catch the next running bus."

"That's two dollars, thirty-nine cents please," Kino said.

"He'll bring it out to you," Poochy tells her as he fills up the condiments under the counter.

"Man, did you see her?" Kino asks.

"Man, did you see you! You look like you saw Meagan Good naked in your bedroom!"

"No, I saw the love of my life, and I'm going to marry her. I don't care how many kids she has!"

"Happy Meal ready," the cook yelled from the back.

"What you going to say?" Poochy asked.

"I don't know."

"Man, give her some extra food."

"What you think I should give her?" asked Kino.

"A Big Mac, then tell her you're her big Mac," as he grabs his groin area like a macho man.

Kino pushes him, telling him no. Then he looks at the canceled drive-through order and sees a fish sandwich and a

Happy Meal. He grabs them, some fries, places the food on a tray and walks out to her. As he gets half way from approaching her, loud music is shaking the walls coming from a truck outside, playing Feel the Bass, by Magic Mike. Kino wonders if she's going to run to the window like every hoochie mamma does, hoping she's not a Trues and Vogue hoe. She looks but she doesn't run, she doesn't even move. Instead, she turns towards Kino with her beautiful smile and startles him, as he trips and falls, knocking over all the food.

She runs over to him and asks, "Are you alright?"

She picks up the food and helps him up. She is cracking up inside, but only giggles. He's embarrassed as fries fall out of his hair. His homeboy Poochy is rolling on the floor with laughter behind the counter, nearly in tears. He recovers quickly and start fixing another tray for her with a Big Mac instead of a fish sandwich.

Kino cleans up the mess and apologizes then gets her food from Poochy, and tells him, "Thanks bro, I owe you one." Kino takes the food out to her.

"This is not my food," she said.

"It's all good, I got this for you."

"OK, if you insist, but I don't eat Big Macs. I like fish sandwiches."

"No problem." Another girl walks in.

"Hey, Tanisha."

"What's up Shawana?"

"You going to the club this Sunday?"

"If my Mom will babysit, you know how she is."

As Kino walks back to get the fish sandwich, Poochy is acting like he just caught the love virus from Kino, as if it's contagious.

"Man, who's her friend? You got to hook us up!" said Poochy.

"I don't know. Take her order and find out." Kino play pushes

Poochy and tells him, "I told you the fish sandwich." Kino yells "fish sandwich" to the cook. "She don't even like Big Macs." When the fish sandwich came up, he brought it out to her.

"Thank you," she said. "Shawana, ain't he such a gentleman, giving me extra food then bringing it out to me?"

Shawana's mouth is too full of food, eating the Big Mac that Kino brought out before. She just waves as she chews away.

"She loves Big Macs, it's her favorite sandwich."

"Kino," calls the Manager.

"I'll holla at yall, I got to go."

"You and Poochy unload the dairy truck, the driver is in the back waiting," the Manager said.

Unloading the truck, Poochy says, "I didn't even get to take her friend's order. Did you get her number?   What's up? When we going on a double date?" Poochy asks, spitting questions back to back, anxiously waiting for an answer.

"No, I didn't get her number, I didn't even get her name."

"What? Are you crazy? We coulda got fired for the extra food we gave her, and you didn't even get her name?" Poochy says.

"No, but her friend loves Big Macs..." said Kino.

"She does?" asked Poochy, replying as if he forgot that Kino didn't get no name or number and they coulda got fired. "I told ya I know what a girl wants," beating himself on the chest like King Kong.

CHAPTER FOUR

Coupe is at the front door of Kino and Murk's house knocking. (knock, knock)

Silence, then harder.

(KNOCK, KNOCK)

"Who is it?"

"It's me, knucklehead."

Murk opens the door saying, "You was about to get blast playing around."

"With what, your cap gun?"

"No, this," Murk said, pointing a Black 9mm Glock at Coupe. "Where you get that from?"

"Don't worry about that, Detective Gadget," Murk said.

"Man, where everybody at?"

'They ain't got off work yet," answered Murk.

The voice of Mrs. Betterman that warms the house when she speaks says, "I left dinner on the stove. Leave that meat in the crock pot on, check it every now and then and just add water if it gets low. That's for tomorrow. I got to go to work. Yall boys be good. There's enough for you too Coupe, if you want to eat."

"Thanks, Mrs. Betterman. "

"Yall behave."

"Yes ma'am," they say simultaneously.

Mrs. Betterman leaves and Coupe beats Murk to the food as they sit at the table and eat.

"She needs to open her own restaurant. These wings off the chain. No fast food chain has nothing on these homemade fries," said Coupe.

"I love that woman. After my mother died I had no one to turn to, and she welcomed me in with a big hug," said Murk.

"I like her too, especially her cooking," replied Coupe.

"Man, you playing. What's up with Super Sunday at Club Silhouette? We going?" asked Murk.

"Yea, what's up with Kino and Poochy? They want to go?

"I don't know."

"I got to go. Ask them what's up, and tell Mrs. B the food was good."

"Aight, I'll holla."

Kino walks in at 11:30 p.m. hungry and tired from work.

"What's up Murk?"

"Your mother."

"What you mean?" Kino asked.

"That slimy man at the car lot trying to repo Mom's car."

"Damn! You got to get a job and help out. I'm already giving

Mom my whole check and that still ain't enough. I'm hungry, what she cooked?" asked Kino.

"The food in the kitchen."

Kino walks in the kitchen and looks in the pan. "What's this? You only left me three small wings. There's not even a handful of my favorite homemade potato fries!"

"It was Coupe, not me," Murk said.

"Coupe don't live here, you do. Why you didn't save me some?"

"I did," said Murk.

"That little bit? Man, you need to get a job!"

"Punk, you need to mind your own business and don't worry about me. I'm a grown man."

"If you're a grown man then help Mama out, you little boy. And stop laying in the house all day eating all the food and save some for the real man of the house. You little boy!", said Kino.

Murk swung on Kino and caught him smack on the jaw and floored him. Kino got up and charged him. Murk threw another blow, but it didn't even phase Kino. Kino football tackled Murk and slammed his head into the wall, then he slammed Murk on the floor, got on top and started swinging on Murk until Murk flipped Kino over. Now they on the floor wrestling back and forth. The door opens. Kino's Mother, Mrs. B came rushing in.

"Stop it! What are yall doing?"
They let each other go, put their heads down and went to their room. Mrs. Betterman cleaned up the mess, sat down, and started crying.

Single Black women left alone to raise the children. When the Black father/husband is taken out of the picture, we leave our beautiful Black Queens alone to raise our children. Now she has to fulfill two positions. Financially support her children and nurture them with her natural motherly love. It's not easy to slave a 9 to 5 then come home, cook, clean for the children and attend to them, like going over their homework, ironing their clothes for tomorrow, fixing their lunches, etc. Me, as a man, from my personal experience, when I come home from a hard day of work I'm not trying to cook no meal and clean behind no kids. I'm too tired. So I tip my hat with the utmost respect and props to that independent mother who's doing it all by herself. We Black men need to value our responsibility to our Lord first and foremost, our wives, parents and children. That is what is important, not money, jewelry, cars, and hoes. Are you not yet tired of seeing your sister, your mother, your daughters, your aunts, your nieces, and your very own wife struggle by themselves with our children while we kill each other and send each other to prison?

Kino went to thinking about his Father, why did he have to catch another charge in prison that gave him twenty more years instead of coming home when Kino was fourteen?

Kino said to himself, "Mom wouldn't be going through this if you were here and I wouldn't have to give my whole check to her and we still broke. It's got to be a better way than this, because McDonald's ain't cutting it."

All Murk could think about was Kino's words - "Help Momma out you little boy!"

Here you have the typical young Black male who has no role model growing up in the house showing him how to be a man. Instead, he learns from a woman who raises him or from the streets. The streets brew many different types of evil men - from gangbangers, to pimps, to dope dealers, to robbers, all of which eventually end up being stock for prisons or coffins at the graveyard, one or the other.

CHAPTER FIVE

Pastor Placky invited Dr. Hamilton, his wife and daughter over for dinner. Dr. Hamilton believes in early marriage. He's an old school, church driven, high-class entrepreneur. He knows that early marriage prevents fornication and children of the bed, bastards, from being born. He wants the best for his daughter and he thinks the preacher's son is the ideal husband for his daughter. Likewise, Pastor Placky thinks Dr. Hamilton's money is good for the church.

The doorbell rings. Mrs. Placky answers the door.

"Welcome Dr. and Mrs. Hamilton. May I ask who is this beautiful young lady?"

"My daughter, Quanita Hamilton."

"She looks the same age as my son, Curtis. Come on in and have a seat." (Curtis, a.k.a. Coupe.)

Pastor Placky walks in.

"Dr. what a pleasure to have you and your family as guests."

"Thank you Pastor, it's our pleasure to be here."

"Curtis," Pastor Placky calls for his son.

"Yes father."

"Come down here and meet Dr. Hamilton, his wife and his beautiful daughter."

Curtis comes downstairs.

"How are you doing sir, ma'am, aanndd ... " He prolongs

the script his father taught him.

"Qaunita is my name."

He takes her hand and walks her over to the seat and pulls her chair out and says, "Please have a seat, Quanita."

Everybody sits down. Pastor Placky needs to make sure everything is going as planned.

"Son, come with me and help me with the appetizers."

They leave the living room and go into the kitchen.

"Coupe, remember your lines son, lawyer not doctor. He wanted to be a lawyer but Mrs. Hamilton changed that."

"I got you dad."

"That's my boy."

They bring out anchovy egg canapes topped with lumpfish caviar. Dr. Hamilton's eyes get big.

"I see Pastor Placky, you have class and know foods. What do you have to drink with this?"

"Chardonnay."

"Pastor Placky, that's for women. I ate dinner with the Senator last week and he showed me a drink to go with appetizers and we had a blast."

"If you don't mind, could you share that with me?"

"Only if you don't mind making it the next time we meet," he says as he smiles.

"I absolutely do not mind."

"OK. It's one and a half ounces of Grey Goose Vodka, one and a half ounces of Cocchi Americano Rosa, a quarter of an ounce of Amaro Ramazzotti, and two dashes of orange bitters. You stir it all together with a little ice, then strain it into a coupe glass, and last, garnish it with a twist of orange peel." Then he steps toward Pastor Placky and whispers, "Take your Viagra then after dinner your wife will love you for the rest of the year."

"Ha! Ha! Ha! Ha! they burst out laughing and give each other high five.   The wives look at each other.

"What yall whispering at?" Mrs. Hamilton asked.

"Nothing honey, just telling him about the night with the Senator ...after dinner."

Mrs. Hamilton starts giggling, "Ooh, I hope you got your refill." She slaps him on the back.

Dr. Hamilton turns to Curtis. "So Curtis, what are you doing with your life?"

Pastor Placky looks Coupe dead in the eyes. It's a look that says, 'if you mess up, I'm going to whoop your ass all night!'

"Well sir, I'm the Captain of Evans High School Debate Team. I do voluntary attorney work for The Debacotti Firm. It doesn't count for intern or college credit. I only do it for experience and building relationships in the judiciary world. My dad says it's all about relationships. So I'm starting now in my senior year, before I go to Harvard or FAMU Law School. I'm supposed to be the Valedictorian this year, but there's a serious murder trial that's coming up. I want all the experience I can receive from that case. To me, my passion to be a lawyer is more important than giving a speech."

The Hamilton's were impressed. The more wine they drunk the looser they got. Quanita sat straight up, shy and quiet, shoulders straight, looking like a prep girl ready to get pluck.

Coupe is thinking to himself, "She's probably a virgin. I'm going to put-it-on-her."

She wore a long sleeve button-up shirt that was button all the way up to the top, matching loose baggie pants and shiny flat round shoes. She attended Bishop Moore Private School, and looked like she never been to a party or a club in her life.

While the parents mingle, Coupe gets acquainted with her, gets her phone number, and sets up a date next week.

The following morning, Mrs. Placky is reading from an article in the morning newspaper. It read:

Alcohol kills more than cocaine, crack, heroin, tobacco, or any kind of drug, and is the number one substance abuse that causes family destruction.

"See, when Jesus turned the water into wine, everything was fine It's what a person chooses to do when they drink, not the drink itself. Wine is a gift from God, and I love my gift from God. In fact, Bae, pour me a glass of chardonnay," said Pastor Placky.

"All that wine you and Dr. Hamilton drank last night, you still want more?

"Haven't you heard? A glass of wine every day keeps the doctor away," he said.

"I thought it was an apple a day keeps the doctor away."

"Well, something like that. Bae, don't fix it in no champagne flute or martini glass, use that highball glass I bought."

"That's a big glass. Next thing you know it will be Grey Goose," Mrs. Placky mumbled under her breath.

"What you said?" he asked.

"Nothing."

"I heard something."

"I said this is the last of the wine."

After his third glass he sits back with a buzz, feeling tipsy, and starts visualizing. He thinks to himself, "T.D. Jakes, that's what I'm talking about, he makes millions. I could be like him and produce my own record. Since I can't sing, I'll get a choir and talk over the beat like Kirk Franklin, that's all Luke does."

Then he sang out loud, "Don't stop, get it, get it." He went back to thinking. "I can do that. I could make movies and have a Mega Fest like T.D. Jakes."

Then he started calculating T.D. Jakes money from his services. "At just two services on Sunday, 20,000 people attend each service. If each person gives up twenty dollars, then that's four hundred thousand every Sunday, or one point six million every month. Even if everybody just gives up ten dollars, or half the people still give up twenty dollars, then that's eight hundred thousand a month, not including services throughout the week, his records, movies and Mega Fest. So this is how Creflo Dollar is able to buy a thirty-million-dollar jet. Forget selling dope and robbing. This way more money."

CHAPTER SIX

Poochy's mother, Mrs. Mable, was trying desperately to save her father's church.   She felt like it was the only thing keeping Poochy's Grandfather alive. One time he opened the mail and it read:

"FORECLOSURE NOTICE"

He had a faint heart attack, fell and bust his head open. He had to receive five stitches.

Reverend Benny was his name. He loved preaching to the have-nots, winos, transits, crack heads, and whoever society would not accept. If one of his attendees was to enter Pastor Placky's church, they might call the police. Mrs. Mabel drew a second mortgage from her house to stop the foreclosure on the church. She has been taking the money from the church to pay the house mortgage, and taking the money for the house mortgage to pay for the church, going back and forth, paying whichever bill comes first. Poochy's father lost his job, so the only income has been the money from the church's donations, and Poochy's check from McDonalds. His mother was a homemaker who busts her butt cleaning the house and church from the bottom to the top.

She took care of her father, her husband and Poochy's younger sister. She cooked for the family every day and whoever comes in from the streets to eat. Poochy's parents were old school, good old Christians, who lived the original

Christian way, where the husband pays all the bills and the wife takes care of the home, her husband, and the kids. They have been struggling since Poochy's father lost his job. So now the church and their house are in jeopardy, along with Grandpa's health. Poochy and his little sister lay in their rooms trying to sleep as they hear an argument through the thin, cheap, hollow walls.

"What am I supposed to do? We 'bout to lose the house and the church."

"I don't know, but please don't go back to your old ways. I would rather have you here broke and alive than to be locked up or dead!" Mrs. Mabel said while trembling and crying. Let's just keep praying and wait on God," said Mrs. Mabel. Tears fall from Poochy's little sister Laquita's eyes, and Poochy punches the headboard of his bed.

"Take your ass to sleep Poochy," yells his Father, who hasn't cursed since he stopped drinking ten years ago.

CHAPTER SEVEN

They pull into the parking lot of Club Silhouette to attend Super Sundays, and parked far away from the crowd, embarrassed to be seen in a 1996 two door Toyota Corolla.

With all of them in the car, it droops to the ground looking like a Puerto Rican' low rider. It rides with three hubcaps, the other rim as Black as the tire, a faded paint job on top, the windows don't roll down and there's no A/C. The front passenger seat doesn't move up nor does the back part of the seat flip forward so that the person in the back seat can get in and out easily, being it's a two door vehicle. If they stop to holla at anybody they have to open the car door just to speak. Coupe's father is a miser, which is why he didn't help Coupe financially buy a better conditioned car. Instead, he handed down to Coupe his old college car, that constantly broke down on him and Coupe's mother.

Murk has no money, as usual. The money that Coupe makes he keeps to himself because he doesn't have to hand over his check to help his parents pay bills. On the other hand, Kino and Poochy have to give up most of their whole check to their Mother. Poochy and Kino both grossed one sixty a week. After taxes, they brought home around one twenty.

Raised in this western society, responsibility of

being a man is nowhere in the mind of a seventeen-year-old. Living in a materialistic environment, chasing money, cars and women easily lead one astray from their priorities in life. When are we going to become men and put our priorities first before chasing dead presidents, fortune and fame?

Squeezing out of the back seat to get out of the car, Poochy says, "Damn, did you see that chick in that Challenger?"

"Where at?" said Coupe.

"The pink one, parked over there, sitting on those pink Diablos. She smashing you Coupe."

"Yall don't even have a car, you got feet. Keep talking and you'll be using them to get home tonight," Coupe says as they all start laughing.

"There she goes hollering at that nigga in the Hummer on thirty-twos. You can't see her body, but she fine like Jhonni Blaze on The Love of Hip Hop New York."

Four Chevy donks, two of them verts, all rolling on twenty eights with candy paint, except one that flip-flop colors rolls through.

They ride real fast then slam on their brakes, making their cars jerk back and forth, swerving left to right, playing Plies first mixtape 36 Ounces. All you see is a bunch of dreads, bald heads, big beards, and gold teeth bouncing up and down, shaking their dreads to the beat with two females with them.

Kino and his click stand in the long line as they watch the show put on by the four Chevy donks. A person standing in line behind them says, "That's Dae'Quan and them niggas from Cross town." They park and get out. Their whole click walks by, passing everybody straight to the V.I. P. Skip Line. As they walk by Poochy yells, "There goes the love of my life. Kino, that's them!"

"Who?" Kino said.

"The girls from work."

"Damn she's sexy," yells Coupe.

Kino's heart jumps and his stomach bubbles with butterflies as they walk pass them.

"Ain't that them same niggas from Cross town driving crazy through the parking lot with them?" asked Murk.

"Hey, how we going to get in? Murk the only one eighteen," asked Coupe.

"Tell them you ain't got no I.D. and they'll just make you pay extra." said Poochy.

The lady behind the window says, "Twenty dollars and your I.D."

"I lost my I.D.," Kino says.

"Forty then," the lady blurts back.

Kino turns around and tells everybody "forty dollars." Murk doesn't have any money, so Kino has to pay his way.

"I have two, one with I.D., and I lost mines," said Kino.

"Sixty dollars," the lady said.

"Show her your I.D.," Kino told Murk.

"I lost my I.D. too," he said.

"Damn! You ain't got no money and no I.D. That's twenty more dollars," said Kino.

"You just a broke-ass nigga," said Coupe.

"Eighty for two with no I.D.," the lady groaned, becoming impatient.

"That's over half my check," Kino thinks to himself.

They all pay then walk in the club. "Damn!" was their response as they walked in and saw a sight they never witnessed before. It's their first time being at Silhouette, which was far different from the hole-in-the-wall teen clubs they had been to.

"Man, every body's here!" said Kino.

"Isn't that Amare Stoudemire," asked Coupe.

"That's got to be him, look how tall he is," replied Kino.

"Marquis Daniel and Warren Sapp supposed to be in here too,"

said Coupe.

"Man, where them girls at? Bump them niggas!" said Poochy. "Everywhere fool, can't you see?" said Coupe.

"I'm talking about the ones from McDonalds," said Poochy. "Probably in V.I.P. with them ballers from Cross town. I want to get drunk," said Murk.

"How you gonna get drunk when you ain't got no money?" asked Coupe.

"Let's chip in on a bottle," suggested Poochy.

"We ain't got no drinking band or enough money for a bottle," said Kino.

"There goes Giovoni, let's get him to buy our drinks," said Murk.

"Aye Giovoni!"

"What y'all jits doing in here?"

"We came to represent the hood bro."

Kino and Murk yell "Meerrcee! Meerrcee!"

Poochy yells "AAA PEE KAAY!"

And Coupe yells "PINNE HILLLLS!"

"OK, Mercy Drive," said Giovoni.

"Murda Drive," Murk responds.

"Could you buy us a drink? We got our own money, we don't have no drinking bands," asks Kino.

"I'll be right back, let me get yall some drinking bands."

"You got pull like that?" Poochy asks.

"It's about money and relations," said Giovoni.

Giovoni walks off. He woulda bought them each a bottle without denting his pockets. Instead, he wanted to see how real they were and if they were going to try to use him for his money. They didn't, so he took a liking to them. Little do they know, Giovoni has money invested in the club as a silent partner. Getting four drinking bands was no problem for him. He comes back with the bands, gives them a dap and spins off.

"It's one of yall turn to foot the bill for Murk," said Kino. Murk is quiet and mad as hell because he's broke with no money in front of his friends.

*****

"Girl, let's walk the club," said Shawana.

"You know Dae'Quan don't want me going nowhere. That's why I didn't want to come with him, but you insisted," said Tanisha.

"Free ride, free drinks, free V.I.P., free balling status," Shawana tells Tanisha.

All for the price of her freedom and happiness, is what Tanisha was thinking. She never really liked Dae'Quan, but she got caught up in the hype of the big dope-boy in the hood with the cars, money, and who all the girls wanted from the hood. Tanisha was young and got caught up when he showered her with money and made her famous by being with her. It was all a show, just a reason to get in her drawers. Unfortunately for her, she got pregnant. He'll spin money on cars and other females before he'll take care of his child.

Tanisha looks at him from a distance as he slaps a girl's ass and walks her and all her friends to the V.I.P. bar.

"Come on Shawana, let's go."

******

"This double shot of Grey Goose got me feeling it," said Coupe.

"That was a double shot? I drunk that like it was a single shot," said Murk.

"You suppose to sip it and make it last. You know we got to have money for gas. We didn't have time to get gas, remember?" said Kino.

"Man, let's take a picture," said Poochy.

There's a Lil Wayne backdrop.   Polaroid poses - giving each other dap, holding their empty cups in the air, flaunting like they got money. They took four different pictures, one for each person.

Coupe sees some girls from the school and grabs them and tells them to flick it up with them. So they take four more pictures.

The music's bumpin', the bass is moving their chests, the crowd is chanting the words of Jeezy - "I went from old school Chevy's to drop top Porsches!"

In their cups is nothing but melted ice, as they sip and suck on the ice and spit it back out in the cup, bobbing their heads feeling tipsy, flaunting as if they were really drinking.

"Can me and my girls take some pictures?" one of the girls from his class asks.

Not wanting to be looked at as a broke chump, Coupe says, "Anything for you boo, I got you."

The girls flick up four more pictures. And all of them are caught up in the moment, not realizing how much money they are spending.

"Sixty dollars," said the cameraman.

"Somebody going to be siphoning for gas tonight Murk," said Coupe.

Little do they know there is fire in Murk's eyes while they are all laughing. He's at a point of exploding, so he walks away. Kino and Poochy put fifteen dollars apiece and Coupe pays the rest.

They turn around just in time to see the groupies grab their pictures, and head to the bar, chasing some ballers.

Murk comes back after cooling off and says, "Man, I need another drink," looking at Kino.

"Me too," says Poochy.

Kino looks at them crazy. He's the only one conscious of spending all his money, but not conscientious enough to remember he was supposed to give his whole check to his Mother for bills.

They go to the other side of the club and by the bar, low and behold, there they go - the women of their dreams.

"Isn't that the boy from McDonald's?" asks Shawana.

"Yes, that's him," replied Tanisha.

Coupe walks right up to Tanisha, bold and very mannish, grabbing her ass saying, "What's up sexy, caramel candy, bootylicious?"

She slapped fire from his face, like she was Giancarlo Stanton hitting a home run. Murk was laughing his ass off. Coupe shook the blow off and was puzzled. Then out of nowhere, on reaction, he cocked his fist back getting ready to throw a blow that would put her to sleep. He swung at her as if she was a man. Before he could strike, Kino jumped in front of her and took the blow, and was floored. Then Murk grabbed Coupe and slammed him intentionally, acting like he was breaking up the fight. On the real, Murk was trying to break his back.

Once again, Kino is on the floor and this beautiful girl is on top of him, holding him. Poochy grabs her friend, the one he's in love with, and says, "I got you, I got you. No one is going to hurt you. I got you."

Kino gets up. "Are you alright?" Tanisha asks.

"Yeah."

"What made you jump in front of me?"

"I couldn't stand to see no one hurt a beautiful woman like you." Tanisha is crying inside because all she ever witness was her Mother getting beat, her girlfriend's man beating them, and her baby daddy abused her as well. No man never stood up for her like that. That's when the love-jones began.

"Let's go sit down," invited Tanisha. Poochy, Shawana, Kino and she sat at a table and got acquainted with each other, exchanged numbers and names.

Murk pushed Coupe away to calm him down. They got back with the girls they were taking pictures with. Coupe spent the rest of his money on drinks for Murk and the four girls.

"Double shot for everybody," yells Coupe, acting like he's a big- time dope dealer. Kino and Poochy tell the waiter, "Two double shots of Grey Goose, and whatever the women want." Kino spends all his money and Poochy has twenty dollars left. Kino tells Poochy, "I got to use the bathroom," and winks at Poochy to follow him.

"I'll be right back, don't go nowhere," Kino tells Tanisha.

"I got to go use the bathroom too," says Poochy.

They get to the bathroom. "I don't have any more money, lend me ten dollars so I can buy her some roses," said Kino.

"Aight."

You know Poochy is not going to let Kino come back with roses and he doesn't have any. So he spends his last twenty dollars on the roses. They both come back with the roses behind their back to surprise them.

"Tanisha, bring your ass over here. Where you been at all night?" yells Dae'Quan. He grabs her arm and pulls her with him. She snatches her arm away from his grip. Dae'Quan draws back to slap the daylight out of her. As soon as he drew his hand back, Kino knocked the daylight out of him. He never saw it coming. Before you knew it, a mass of niggas was on Kino and Poochy's ass.

Dae'Quan's click saw Kino and Poochy sitting with Tanisha and Shawana. So they told Dae'Quan, which is why he came to get her. Poochy tried to fight the goons off Kino, but before he knew it, there were just as many goons on him as there were on Kino.

Two chairs are thrown at the wolves surrounding Kino and Poochy. All you see is a nigga with dreads crashing chairs on people's backs who are stomping on Kino. It's Murk. Coupe waits until the bouncers come and break it up, then he gets all wild and crazy acting like he's going to kill someone as the bouncers throw him out.

No one knows that Coupe is a scaredy-cat, and didn't do anything but throw that one chair from far away. On the contrary, Murk was smashing chairs on people's back then started fighting them. Eventually, they all get thrown out and end up back in the car all together. Coupe cranks up the car.

"Who was those niggas and what the hell happened?" asked Coupe.

Then he looks at the gas gauge.   "Man, we on "E" and I don't have no money. "

"Neither do I," said Kino.

"I'm broke too," Poochy said.

 "Let me out. I got to use the bathroom," said Murk

"Where you going?" asked Kino.

"Behind this building to piss."

When he gets behind the building out of their view, he runs to the other side of the parking lot where he sees a group of women walking back to their car. He thinks for a moment, then he looks across the street at the hotel that's behind Wet-N-Wild on International Drive. Murk runs over there discretely, and the first White female he sees is his victim. He ducks, squats behind a car, takes off his shirt, ties it around his head and face like a Taliban wrap, with nothing but his eyes showing. He runs full speed at her, snatches her purse, and hauls ass back across the street.

The woman fainted at the sight of a strong young Black man with a masked face running full speed at her. She thought he had a gun, got scared and passed out. The woman is on the ground unconscious so no one sees anything unusual besides Murk running in a tank top. He has the purse wrapped in his shirt where the other people can't see it.

Back in the club parking lot people looked at him crazy. Some of the scared dudes went ducking and dodging, but most of the parking lot pimps went reaching for their fire ready to blast Murk if he came at them. By the time he gathered his composure and put his shirt back on, he looked back and saw a few people surrounding the lady on the ground. He walked back to the car and gets in the back seat.

"I know you didn't," Kino says as he sees Murk with a purse. As they crank up and ride away they see the police running across the street to the commotion at the hotel. Kino and the crew drive away.

CHAPTER EIGHT

Poochy walks in the house from the club bruised up with a swollen face. It's four a.m., and as soon as he walks in, his little sister football tackles him with a big hug and starts crying.

"Daddy beat Mommy," she said.

"What happened?" Poochy asked.

He walks into the kitchen to see his Mother sitting at the table. There are tears coming down her eyes, her nightgown is ripped and her hair is mangled, her head is hanging down. He sees an ice bag in her hand. Poochy runs to her.

"MOM!"

She looks at him. and low and behold, she has a Black eye.

"Where he at Mom?"

"He left."

"Why! Why! All you do is care for him, me, Laquita, Grandpop, and anyone who walks up to the church. You don't deserve this Mom."

She's gasping for words, stuttering and crying at the same time, trying to talk.

"He started back drinking. He couldn't take it no more. Your Father was tired of not being able to take care of his family."

Mrs. Mabel still makes excuses for him like she used to ten years ago. Poochy's Father was a stone-cold killer and robber. He would tie a person up, torture them, and take everything they have. He would only do it when he was drinking. Alcohol is the devil to Poochy's Father. He's been alcohol-free for ten years, and now he started back. A decade later things are not the same. Everybody is strapped and the robbers are getting murked. People are not scared these days.

CHAPTER NINE

Mrs. B. (Mrs. Betterman) already knew her car was going to be repoed. So the money she had for the car note she used to catch up the rent she was behind on. She doesn't get paid again until Monday. That check is for the rent, but now she can use that money, plus Kino's money, to get the car out of repo.

"Knock, knock," Mrs. B knocking on Kino and Murk's bedroom door.

"Wake up, breakfast ready waiting on yall. Time to get up and go to school."

"What time is it?" asks Kino.

"Time for you to get your butt up. I need that money to get the car out of repo." Kino felt like his head was hit by a sledgehammer when she said that. Murk's heart dropped. They both forgot all about the money Kino was supposed to give to his Mother to help with the bills.

"What happened to you Kino? Why is there blood on these sheets? And your face is swollen."

"Mom, I got into a fight in the club and, and, and..."

"And what?"

"I don't have the money. "

"I can't believe this. Murk, did you drag him into this? I've been busting my ass working, going to school, trying to send money to your father, and taking care of you two. I clean up behind yall, I cook for yall every night after school and work. And you go out, spend all your money, get into a fight, come home drunk, and now you want to skip school? My car was repoed last night. So how am I supposed to go to work, and then get to school on time? I can't do it on the bus. I'll be late and will miss class and get kicked out or leave work early and get fired."

She slams the door and walks away crying. Murk looks at Kino and Kino looks at Murk. Both feeling like a piece of manure. There were only twenty dollars in the purse Murk snatched and a few credit cards. He gave the twenty dollars to Coupe for gas. Broke, busted and disgusted with themselves, Kino's body is sore from the feet stomping on him and his lip is swollen. Murk's pride and feelings have him near suicide or going off on a terrorist rampage. There's no telling what he might do.

CHAPTER TEN

D-Bo was supposed to come home when his son Kino turned fourteen. Allah Ta'Ala, God The Most High, decreed a different plan. D-Bo caught a murder charge in prison that gave him twenty more years.

Two knees on the floor, elbows on the bed, hands closed together. "Dear Jesus or God please help me. I want to change my life and become closer to you."

In search of guidance from the Creator, D-Bo walks the track with two Christians. "D-Bo, Jesus is your Lord and Savior. He died on the cross for your sins. John 3:16 says, *"God so loved the world that he gave his only begotten son, that whosoever believed in him should not perish, but have everlasting life."*

"Believe in him how?" asked D-Bo.

"That he died on the cross for your sins."

"So if I believe that he died on the cross for my sins, you saying that I will not perish and have eternal life?"

"Yes, if you believe that and that Jesus is the Son of God, and that he rose from the dead, you will go to heaven for eternity."

"I don't understand why God's son has to die for you and my wrong doings when we had a choice to do wrong or right. That's not just or fair to Jesus, nor does it make any sense when God Almighty has the authority to forgive those who repent sincerely," replied D-Bo.

"D-Bo, back in the old days, which you will find in the Old Testament, animals were sacrificed for your sins. Jesus was the final sacrifice for your sins. Jesus was the final sacrifice for everybody's sins. So that now if you sin and you believe that Jesus died on the cross for your sin, you do not have to sacrifice an animal to God, and you will go to heaven for eternity," said one of the Christian brothers.

"I heard one of those Muslims saying that Allah is the Most Merciful and Oft-Forgiver. All you have to do is repent sincerely to Allah and according to His will, He will either punish you or forgive you for He is the Most High and able to do all things," D-Bo replied.

"Don't believe them.   Look at them praying all the time all over the rec yard. They don't believe in Jesus. Every terrorist act committed on T.V. is always done by a Muslim. And the Black Muslims here in America are racist. They say the White men are devils and the Black men are gods. And if you're not Muslim, they don't care nothing about you," the other Christian brother said.

D-Bo thought to himself. "Muslims don't believe in Jesus. Man, they're crazy. My Grandmother taught me to pray to Jesus and thank Jesus for everything good that happens to me. Jesus was all we had growing up. I believe in my Grandma." He tells his Christian brother, "Yeah, they crazy if they don't believe in Jesus." In the past, the seriousness and unity among the Muslims drew D-Bo toward them. But now since he thought they didn't believe in Jesus, he became less interested in their belief and way of life.

CHAPTER ELEVEN

Phone ringing, Shawana answers.

"Hello."

"What's going on?"

"Who is this?"

"This King Poochy lil momma."

"Boy, I'm sooo so sorry."

"What in the hell was all that about? And who were them niggas?"

"They from Crosstown."

"Who was that punk that was gonna slap Tanisha?"

"Her baby-daddy. "

"Well why she hollering at my boy when she knows her man is in the building?" Poochy's thinking to himself ... "*It's women like this who get men in trouble. They think they're two-quarters slick and have all the sense. Hoes like her will get a brother killed or locked up for killing one of her ducks.*"

"That's not her man," Shawana told Poochy.

"Well what in the hell you call that?"

"She was only using him so he could pay our way in the club, V.I.P. and free drinks."

"So she a gold digging-ass hoe."

"That's just her baby-daddy and no more. Enough about her. What's up with me and you?"

"I don't know; they say birds of feather flock together. Are you a gold digging-ass hoe too?"

Shawana is flat out deceiving Poochy to conceal the truth. Which is, that it was she who persuaded Tanisha to go with Dae'Quan for financial benefits in the club that night, while in fact Tanisha didn't want to have anything to do with Dae'Quan.

"Boy stop playing with me. I told you what's up. There's only one way to find out. I'm ready when you're ready, to answer your question."

"OK, if you not a gold digging hoe, then take me out on a date, all expenses paid by you," Poochy told her.

"Whaaaaat you say?" she asks stuttering.

"Yoooou heeeeeard me," he stutters back, imitating her.

"OK."

"So what we gonna do?" asked Poochy.

"Go on a picnic."

"A picnic?"

"I'm taking you on a date, so I pay, I choose."

"Aight. I'm gonna see what you're about."

Phone call to Tanisha

Phone ringing.

"Hello."

"What's up?"

"Who this?"

"Kino." He had call-blocked his number.

"Why are you just now calling me? I've been worried and thinking about you. Why you didn't answer or return my calls? Are you all right?" asked Tanisha.

"I'm alive, even though your man and his boys were sure trying to kill me."

"He's not my man, he just my baby-daddy."

"That's even worse. He sure wasn't acting like he wasn't your man.   Why you ain't tell me you got a man and he was in the club?"

"I told you, he ain't my man."

"Then what do you call it?" Kino asked.

- pause on the phone -

"What's wrong, the cat got your tongue? I don't need no tricking-ass hoe playing games with me," Kino told her.

She starts crying on the phone and yells out, "Fuck you!" and hangs up.

His heart jumps. He's more hurt than mad, and if you asked him would he do it all again for her, he'd say "hell yeah, in a heartbeat." In fact, he'll take a bullet for Tanisha, because he's in love with her, and she's in love with him too. He's in his feelings and talks to himself, *"Hell no that bitch hung up on me."* Kino knows damn well he wants to call her back, but his pride won't let him.

Tanisha made a poor choice for who she let get in between her legs. How many women, if they could take it back, would have never chosen the baby-daddy they have for their children?

Here we have the typical female who has no help in deciding her spouse or she might have the wrong type of guidance from the wrong people. You Mother's need to watch who you bring around your children, especially if you have girls. If you get a no good lazy-ass bum who doesn't do anything, who doesn't take care of his responsibilities, and your daughter grows up watching you love him, cook for him, take care of him, and accept his sorry ass; then don't be surprised when your daughter grows up and accepts any bum-ass nigga who looks decent and lays pipe to her. If you settle for a man who beats you, then your daughter will too. And the crazy thing about it is, that she will not only settle for a woman beater, but she'll want him to beat her. Some readers might say I'm crazy, but I've seen it. There are some women who get with a man who does not beat her, and she doesn't even want him. She wants the maniac who drags her through the streets and whoops her ass. No lie, I even had a woman tell me, "Why don't you just slap me?" because I tried to walk away.

CHAPTER TWELVE

Coupe is on his first date with Dr. Hamilton's daughter, Quanita. They rode out to Daytona Beach, parked at a hotel, then walked on to the beach. He lays a blanket out on the sand. They find a spot furthest away from the boardwalk where it's quiet and there's little to no people around, if any.

"Look how beautiful the moon is," said Quanita.

"So what you like to do?" asked Coupe.

"Dance and get high."

"Is that why you wanted me to bring this little jukebox, so you can dance for me?"

"Do you know my daddy would kill me if he knew I was dancing?"

"Your daddy is gonna want to kill me when I get through with your ass."

"You are a preacher's son. My daddy should not have to worry about you. It's me he should be worried about." She giggles then pulls out a crystal rock looking substance.

"What's that? I know that ain't no crack," asked Coupe.

"Hell no, it's molly, and this is ecstasy," as she holds up a transformer.

Coupe thinks to himself, "I don't know what this molly is, but I heard that with ecstasy I could sex her all night. I need to try that."

"Where the drink at?" she asks.

He pulls the drink out of the bag along with some ice,

plastic cups, and the radio. She tells him to put the Plies CD in.

"What song?" Coupe asks.

"Hypnotized, featuring Akon."

He grabs a red plastic cup then puts a few ice cubes in it. "I got cranberry and pineapple juice, which one?" he asks her.

"None," she answered.

"Damn, you a soldier. You like it straight on the rocks?" He pours the Grey Goose in the cup and hands it to her, then pours himself a cup.

"Let me take that pill, you can have that molly," said Coupe. "I'm already eating, I'm gonna put the rest in my drink, and sip on it. This your first pill?" she asked Coupe.

"Hell no," he answered.

Coupe lying his ass off, afraid of being embarrassed by having Miss Upper-class Doctor's Daughter showing him the ropes. He feels like he's the street person, because he hangs out on Mercy Drive with Kino and Murk and hangs in Apopka with Poochy. He's really from the last part of Pinehills that turned Black. He still has White neighbors, and the only Blacks that live near his house are middle-class Blacks. Even though Pinehills is quickly turning ghetto.

"Then you can handle the whole pill, because beginners should start off with half," she told him.

"Give me that whole pill, you just make sure you can handle what I bring on this pill."

Plies' song comes on. "*You got me so hypnotized the way your body rolling round and round, that booty keep bumpin' ass just bouncing up and down.*"

"That's my song," she shouted.

She takes her clothes off down to her G-string panties and bra. Coupe popped the whole pill and starts sipping on the Grey Goose. He's sitting up on the blanket. After taking off her clothes, she puts the song on repeat then stands over him and places her hands on her knees, bending over with her buttocks five inches away from his face, and starts poppin' it.

Everything starts spinning to Coupe. It's one buttock in his face, but he thinks it's two, because she makes one side move at a time to the beat, from left to right, the right to left, as she makes each side jiggle individually. Then she stands all the way up and takes her bra off while she's moving to the beat. Now he sees two breasts and he says to himself, "I know a woman has two breasts, so that's one girl." Then he yells out, "What happen to the other girl?"

She pays no mind to him and keeps dancing. Dancing stimulates her hormones and makes Quanita horny, and the molly only intensifies her hormones. She's ready to see what Coupe is going to bring so she dances into position to have sex. From standing, she jumps into a split, landing perfectly on top of him. Then she rolls over on her back, on beat, wiggling her body and winding her G-string off. Now on her back, she raises her legs with one hand on each foot as she spreads her legs back into a split position. All Coupe hears is Akon singing, "*You got me so hypnotized the way your body rolling round and round.*"

He looks and sees her moving each butt cheek separate from the other while she's on her back with her legs in the air. Then he says, "Not again."

She starts slapping the top of her vagina, the clitoris, to the beat, in rhythm. With each kick of the beat, she slaps. Whenever she would stop slapping it, Quanita would place her finger on the little man in the boat, then move her fingers in a circular motion to the beat, going back and forth between these two self-sexual acts. She moves her hand in a circular motion, then stops to slap it, then goes back to the circular motion again, all to the rhythm of the beat. She adds a third act to the show, spreading her eagle as her whole body pauses, becoming still like a statute, except her vagina, as it opens and closes, opens and closes, all to the beat of the music.

Each time her vagina opened, Coupe thought he saw someone standing in there, so he said, "What the fuck!"

Then she said, "I want to fuck too."

Then he got close up on it as she made it open and close, and when he got right up on it as it opened he saw a silver-back gorilla jump at him. Coupe screamed and ran as far and as fast as he could away from her, into the ocean, his clothes, sneakers and all!

CHAPTER THIRTEEN

Dressed in all black, black skully, black shades, Black boots and a Black 9mm Glock placed in a Black book bag, Murk catches a bus to "Drive Now Pay Later" car lot. He's been lying in the bushes for an hour since the car lot closed. The last employee just left, the owner is still in there alone. Murk called his twin sister Precious, and told her to meet him at the car lot. She gets dropped off.

The only thing different between them is that she's a female and he's a male. Other than that, they are identical both in looks and in personality. If Murk were Clyde, Precious would be Bonny, without the intimacy between them. They both had the same rough life. Precious would do anything for Murk. She was the reason why he went to prison. Their Mother's husband tried to rape Precious. As she yelled "Get off me!" Murk came through the door with a metal bat and damn near knocked his head off his body, sending him to sleep. He pulled out his pocket knife and continued to stab him until Murk thought he was dead. He was only twelve years old. Nobody believed the kids. They were both problem children, always getting in trouble. The system punished Murk and let the maniac go, thereby turning Murk and his sister into very resentful and disoriented children.

"When this nigga comes out," Murk says, referring to the car lot owner, "I need you to get him back into his office and make him get butt-ass naked and away from his gun," Murk told Precious.

"I got you bro! He always looking at me when Diamond

and I come up here to pay her car payment." Diamond is Precious' roommate. They strip and sell their goodies for a living.

Murk lays low in the bushes while the owner locks the office door and gets into his car. He pulls up to the gate, gets out to roll it back, then he sees Precious walking up toward him.

"Damn! What's up Precious? What you doing up here this late?" said Marlon Carmichael.

"I just got into a fight with a customer from the club and he put me out of his car. That was the last straw. I'm not dating him no more. I was hoping you was still here so I could use your bathroom. I really can't hold it no more. "

"Sure, come on in. Let me close this gate back."

What a sucker. He's only thinking about getting into her drawers. They say a woman, or shall I say a vagina, is a man's weakness. They go into the office, he turns off the alarm and she uses the bathroom then comes out.

"Can I use the phone?" she asks.

"What, you need a ride? I'll take you for a small price?" He knew she was a stripper, so he just wanted to pay for this young tenderoni. Precious don't even play when it comes to making money, that's all she knows and what she does.

"And what price would that be?" she responded.

"You take care of me, and I'll take care of you," he says while rubbing his hand down her back to her ass.

"One hundred dollars for head, two hundred and fifty dollars for my goodies."

"How about three hundred for everything?" She laughs, rubbing her hand down his chest to his penis, grabbing it and massaging it, making it rock hard.

"What is this, a negotiation date?" she said giggling.

"I'm just trying to have fun boo. I know you want to get paid, so what's up?"

"OK, but three things."

"What is that?"

"Money first. Go wash your dick second. I'm not sucking

no dirty funky dick, and third I want to hear some music." He goes to the safe, opens it up and takes three hundred dollars out of it, then pushes it closed. He's so much in a rush he doesn't even realize that it didn't close all the way. He gives her the three hundred dollars and turns on the music, and rushes to the bathroom to wash his dick. That's when she rushes to unlock the front door and makes it back before he comes out of the bathroom.

"Are you ready for Big Dick Willie?" he yelled coming out from the bathroom.

"I love me some big dick."

"Why don't you have your clothes off?" he asked.

"I want you to take them off after I suck the hell out of your big dick. Sucking dick turns me on and my clothes don't come off until I'm turned on."

He walks out in his boxers with his pistol in his hand. She rushes to him and grabs his manhood, then pulls it while she leads the way to the desk. She positions him against the wall and starts jacking his dick as she squats down, looking at it eye to eye. She strokes it one time from the top to the bottom. As her hand slides up to the top of his penis, she places her mouth on the head. In harmony together, in a slow stroking motion, as her hand slides down, so does her mouth.

She's a master at this. Precious is a professional. She spits saliva all on the dick making it slimy and wet. She never stops stroking it. As her hand gets slimy it gets in her throat deeper, as she starts slurping and making gushy sounds and breathing hard, saying, "My pussy is getting wet. Grab my hair with both your hands."

He's not even thinking about holding that pistol any longer as he puts it down, takes both of his hands and starts caressing her head, slightly pulling it while she deep-throats his dick with no hands. Sucking it in different ways, she starts back jacking and sucking it at the same time. His eyes roll back as he starts to climax. Murk has been watching through the window and when he saw the man put the pistol down, he eased on through the front door. Marlon could not hear the door open because of the music, nor could he see because, for one, his eyes were rolled back and two, Precious had turned him around with his back toward the door.

She tells him, "I love this dick," as she takes deep breaths and sighs while deep-throating it. When he hears her seductive voice, it turns him on even more.

"I'm about to nut, it's coming!" he yelled.

(click, click) "Hold that nut fuck-nigga!" Murk slaps him with the pistol. Precious stands up and goes straight to the safe.

"Give me your book bag."

"For what?"

"Just give it to me." Murk looks and sees the safe and throws her the bag.

"Fuck -nigga you want to try my Mom, Mrs. Betterman, like she's a prostitute! "(POW) Murk shot him right in the nuts. "Then you go and repo her car!" (POW POW) Two shots to the head, now he's dead. He grabs the lot owner's pistol. She grabs the money and they leave. They catch a cab to Precious' and Diamond's place. Close to eleven thousand dollars they count. A little over five grand a piece they split.

Mrs. Betterman wakes them up the following morning. "Get up, wake up," she says, as she knocks first then opens the door. "Hurry up and eat yall breakfast. I cooked scrambled eggs, turkey sausage, homemade blueberry pancakes with walnuts in them, and strawberry syrup. The orange juice is in the refrigerator. Since I have to catch the bus, I have to leave an hour and a half early. She kisses both of them on the forehead and says, "I love yall but get up! Then she snatches the covers off both of them and leaves. Kino takes a deep breath as he inhales the smell of turkey sausage and it filters through his nostrils making his stomach growl. He says to himself, "I got the best Mom."

Murk was trying to surprise her, but he couldn't wait and he yells, "MOM!" before she exits the front door.

"What? I got to go, I can't miss the bus."

"Come here!"

"This better be important," she said with seriousness in her voice as she walks back into the room.

"How much more do you owe on the 'car?"

"Three thousand dollars and another five hundred to get it out of repo. Why?"

"Well God has been good to you. Here goes thirty-five hundred to pay for the car so you won't have to worry about catching the bus no more. "

"Boy, where you get that money from?" she asks.

"Playing the Lotto Mom. I hit the cash three." She screams, runs and hugs Murk and starts crying.

"Mom, don't start that, you're going to make me cry," Murk said. A tear already fell out of Kino's eye. Murk is fighting the tears back, but when Kino jumped up out of the bed and hugged Murk and his Mother, he started to sob. Murk joined the crowd as the three of them stood together in a group hug of tears of happiness.

CHAPTER FOURTEEN

Since Coupe doesn't have to give his money from his job to his parents, he always has money to spend while Murk, Poochy and Kino are always broke.

> Everything is always OK when you're the only one with money and everyone else is broke. Real G's don't roll like that. Old school gangsters know that when everybody is tight then everybody is happy. The better your click is, the better off you are. We are all one second away from going from rich to poor, free to being locked up, alive and breathing to six feet under. So don't ever take anything for granted. Always have someone to fall on when you're down. But if you are the only one tight, who are you going to fall on when you go down? Because what goes up must come down, and you're not always going to be on top.

"Ride with me to Men's Closet so I can buy an outfit for Lake Lorna Doone," said Coupe.

"You know we ain't got no money for an outfit," said Kino. "Yall can help ME pick ME out an outfit," replied Coupe.

"I need to go to the store anyway for Mom and get some bread and milk," said Kino. Riding to the store Murk is saying to himself, "I'm gonna show this nigga." Kino knows or thinks that Murk hit the cash three Lotto, but he figured he gave it all to Mom, and doesn't have any money left.

They walk into the store and were greeted by the salesman. "What's up people, what can I do for you?" said the salesman. "Let me get the tightest outfit you have," replied Coupe.

Coupe only has two hundred dollars and he thinks he's balling. "Here we have some True Religion Jeans for two hundred and fifty dollars, the matching shirt for a hundred and fifty. You can rock it with this Herman belt for two hundred and these Timberland boots for a hundred. That's roughly seven hundred dollars. I'll tell you what, because you're the coolest dude to walk through those doors today, I'll let you take it all home for an even five hundred." Kino, Poochy and Murk look at Coupe to see what he's going to do.

"I don't want to shine on my friends too hard, so I need something a little cheaper. I don't want to stick out like a sore thumb," said Coupe. Kino and the others burst out laughing.
"Nigga stop flossin like you got it like that," said Murk.
"I know you ain't talking Mr. Can't Pay Your Way in the club or buy a drink, ole broke-ass nigga," said Coupe.
"I got your broke ass. Aye, get me three of those outfits, each one different for me and my boys," said Murk.

Poochy's eyes got big, Kino went to thinking how much money did he win? The most he ever knew for a person to win on cash three was five thousand dollars. He went to adding it up in his head. He gave Mom thirty-five hundred and these three outfits at five hundred a piece is the fifteen hundred he has left.

"You don't have to do this Murk," said Kino.
"It's fine with me. Murk, you the man," said Poochy.
"How is your broke ass going to pay for it?" Coupe says

with a smirk smile on his face.

"With this," said Murk. He pulls out a knot. Kino is looking at the money saying to himself, "That don't look like no money from the bank. What in the hell Murk done did?"

Coupe ends up buying some Levi jeans, a White T-shirt, a Nike hat and a no-name brand belt. He rocked a pair of Jordans he already owned in his closet.

They headed back to the crib to eat and get dressed for the scene at Lake Lorna Doone.

Kino and Murk walk in the house.

"Food is on the stove for yall. Kino, why didn't you read that letter from your Father?" asked Mrs. B.

"I don't want to read it," answered Kino.

"You shouldn't be like that Kino."

"He shouldn't have left us Mom."

Kino grabs the letter, goes to thinking while Murk fixes him a plate of oxtails and rice and sits at the table and starts eating. Kino goes to his room, slams the door, and sits down holding the letter in his hand. His emotions flare up. He thought his Father was coming home when he would turn fourteen. Mrs. Betterman brought him to every visit she could bring him to for thirteen years straight. At visitation, D-Bo would play with Kino. He sat in his Father's lap every visit for years until the guard told him he was too big to do that with him anymore. Kino also used to sit on his Father's shoulders, then he would place his hands on D-Bo's head and act like D-Bo was a car and Kino was steering him by turning his head left or right.

Whichever way Kino would turn his Father's head; D- Bo would go that way. His father would swing him, tickle him, hug him and kiss him and his Mother. They would take pictures together. Even though D-Bo was locked up, the time they did spend was very valuable. Who is to say that if D-Bo was out he might not have spent that true quality time with Kino because he would've been chasing tricks, chasing money, ripping and running the streets. D-Bo was Kino's superhero. All of these things drew Kino close to his Father, so when he turned fourteen, he was waiting that whole year for D-Bo to come home. Then his Father caught another charge that gave him twenty more years. His parents never told him what happened or what the charge was. Kino hasn't talked to his Father or read any of his letters since he was fourteen.

The typical Black family in the hood. We as Black men do not realize the damage we do to our families when we put ourselves in a predicament to be taken away from them for years or even for decades. Our parents are getting old and it's our time to take care of them. Allah, God-Almighty, says in the Qur'an 17:23, 24 –

> *"And your Lord has decreed that you worship none but him. And that you be dutiful to your parents. If one of them or both of them attain old age in your life, say not to them a word of disrespect, nor shout at them, but address them in terms of honor. And lower to them the wing of submission and humility through mercy, and say: My Lord! Bestow on them Your Mercy as they did bring me up when I was young."*

Your parents took care of you when you couldn't take care of yourself. Meaning, when you were a baby, a young boy, and even a grown man, and especially those who are incarcerated. So now when they get old, how are we as men going to return that responsibility ordained by your Creator to them if we are locked up?

Do we think about the damage we do to our wives? Allah, God Almighty, says in the Qur'an 4:34 *"Men are protectors and maintainers of women ..."*

The Prophet Muhammed, Peace and Blessings be upon him, said:

"...their right (your wives) is that you should treat them well in the matter of food and clothing."

How are we as men going to protect our women and maintain them by providing food, clothing and security if we are locked up? Look at what Mrs. Betterman is going through. We as men also have this obligation to the women in our families who are not married. Our Sisters, Mothers, Daughters, Grandmothers, Aunts, Cousins, and Nieces. The female is the man's responsibility to protect and maintain.

When it comes to our children, not only are we obligated to financially support them, but we are also obligated to guide them and be an example to them. We are obligated to teach them about the Creator and that He is the Most High, the only one worthy of being worshiped. If we do not teach them this the streets will teach them to worship other things besides the Creator (shirk), as will society.

Our daughters look at their Fathers as role models of who they want to spend the rest of their lives with. What may sound crazy is that if we are not in our son's lives, they still want to be like us, even if they hate us. So how are we going to guide our children if we're locked up? If we don't guide them, then the streets, T.V., rap music, or any Tom, Dick and Harry will guide them. This is the importance of the damage we do when we are incarcerated.

Kino's eyes get watery as he sits in silence holding the unopened letter, thinking about what it would be like if his Father was home. He throws the letter down and fixes himself something to eat, and then gets dressed.

****

Whether it's for basketball courts, baseball fields, pavilions, barbeques, plastic cups for liquor to drink, weed, women, cars, trucks, motorcycles, thugs, gangsters, pimps, tricks, strippers, dope dealers, college students, old G's, nine-to-five workers, big belly pregnant women, or even baby-mommas with their babies, everybody goes to Lake Lorna Doone on Sunday to stunt, floss and show off whatever one has for others to see. Cars are getting detailed, hair and nails are getting done, outfits are being bought. There's a quarter-mile strip of driving along a two lane road, you can loop back around until you decide to park. First come, first serve park in the center of attention. Late comers only ride through or have to park far away from the strip and walk back up to the center of attention.

Coupe's car had been acting up lately. It cuts off for some reason. When it does, he has to pop the hood and tap the battery cables, wiggle them, or get a jump.

"Don't ride through the strip Coupe, let's take the back road, park back there and walk up," said Kino.
"Let's just ride through one time and then park," replied Coupe.
"What if the car cuts off, what are we going to do?" asked Kino. "It's not going to cut off, it's only a quarter mile, a five-minute
drive. We'll ride through and park on the other side," said Coupe.

When they turned onto Tampa Avenue from Colonial Drive, they couldn't see the park or the crowd. But as soon as they crossed over Old Winter Garden Road, the traffic was backed up. They turned by the lake and just that quick they got caught up in a traffic jam. They can't turn around, it's too crowded. Plus, now they are caught up in the moment of excitement and forget all about the car problems. They are trying to make it to the strip where the crowd of people are hanging out. Cars parked on both sides of the road. The closer they get to the crowd, the slower the traffic moves.

"You hear the drop coming out that Escalade truck?" said Poochy.

"I think he got Giovoni," said Coupe.
"I think so too," said Kino.

They ride by the Escalade SUV with the back seat taken out. Nothing but thirty, twelve-inch kickers with ten Rockford Fosgate, twenty-five hundred watt amps sitting on thirty inch Savini Diamonds. His music keeps setting off the car alarm three cars over.

The scene was a lot of excitement for these young up comers. Alarms were going off, SUV trucks bumping like a concert, verts riding by them at the same time, jamming with twelve, twelve-inch woofers. You hear Rick Ross here, Lil Wayne there, Plies over there, Boosie and Webbie, all playing at the same time. Everybody is jamming, everybody is balling. There are females everywhere.

Kino and them are ready to get out and walk around in their seven hundred dollar outfits. They really don't want to be seen in the lowrider Toyota Corolla. They are now in the middle of the strip, halfway through, and it's been thirty minutes on a five-minute drive. That Cadillac with the thirty twelves didn't even have it all the way up. He popped in that Rich Gang song called "Life Style," and cranked it up. If I didn't know any better, I woulda thought it was a concert. He shut down any and everything else, drowning out their music.

All you see are chicks standing on the hood of their cars, standing up in the beds of trucks, all in the streets, sides of the streets and even sitting in their cars, poppin' that pussy to the beat. Every time the beat drops they drop it low. You see all the niggas singing alone, yelling "*Life Style*," shaking their dreads, jumping up and down. Everything came to a complete stop while that song played. It was a party in the street. Kino, Murk and Poochy get out of the car and start rapping the words, moving their right hands up and down like they're the ones rapping the song in a concert on a stage. Murk starts slinging his dreads like he's a maniac, ready to kill something. Kino just swerves back and forth to the beat, smooth, like an old G. Poochy gets out of the car and starts poppin'. Kino stops dancing and says, "Nigga, what the hell you doing?" Murk busts out laughing. Coupe can't shine because everybody is dressed better than him. And there's this other problem he's thinking about that no one else is yet aware of. The song went off and everything went back to moving.

"Why we ain't moving Coupe?" yells Poochy.

"I told you Coupe," said Kino.

The gap between Coupe's car and the car in front of him gets bigger and bigger to the point where the chicks in a plum colored Magnum rolling on twenty twos behind them start blowing the horn. (beep! beep! beep!)

"We got to get a jump," said Coupe.

"Who's going to jump us?" asks Kino.

"We can't get one here," said Murk.

They could only push the car five feet at a time, then wait a few minutes for the car in front of them to move, then push again for a few feet and wait some more minutes again, because that's how slow the traffic was moving. Every time they stopped for those few minutes, they noticed that all eyes were on them. Not because they had an exotic car for people to look at, but only to be the laughing stock of the Bozo Show.

Murk sees some niggas pointing and laughing with some chicks. He goes in the back seat and pulls that Glock out then starts walking toward them when Giovoni steps out of nowhere in front of Murk and grabs him. The dudes had their backs turned laughing and key-keying with the chicks about to get busted on.

"Chill out Murk! " he says as he grabs him and walks him back to the car. "What's up youngsters?" ask Giovoni.

"Man, we messed up," said Kino.

"What's wrong with the car?" asks Giovoni.

"We need a jump," said Coupe.

"You got cables?" asks Giovoni.

"Naw," Coupe replies.

"Yall jitterbugs off the chain. How is it that you know your car isn't right and you don't have no cables?"

A gap starts to build again between Coupe's car and the one in front of him. "Beep! beep! beep!" from the girls behind them.

Giovoni walks over to the girls, and when they see that it's him they scream and get out and hug him. He tells them to chill and be patient. They say alright and stop blowing their horn. Then he walks over to the on-coming traffic and talks to the driver in the first car. He shakes his head from left to right. He goes to the car behind them and says something. The driver bobs his head up and down, and they give each other a dap. The car then pulls up, hood to hood to Coupe's car. They pop their hoods, get some jumper cables out and jump Coupe's car.

CHAPTER FIFTEEN

Murk wore his outfit all day Sunday and here it is the next day and he puts it right back on. He catches the bus to see his probation officer. He steps on the bus in a seven-hundred-dollar outfit with all eyes on him. Whispers from the onlookers on the bus.

"He must be up to something ... I know this nigga has a car with all that money he wearing." "What is he doing on the bus?" they say amongst each other. They whisper to each other, but little do they know Murk is holding no more than five dollars to his name.

Why do we as Black people become a spendthrift when we receive a lump sum of money? We do not invest or save or buy something of value. Instead, we will dump fifty thousand dollars on a two-thousand-dollar car that we own. Then turn around and sell it for half, if that, of what we have invested in it, or we will ride it until it falls apart and becomes worthless. We will do stupid things like pay ten thousand dollars for a paint job, but have to jump start the car every time we crank it up. My Stepfather owned a paint shop. There would be cars we painted that we had to push into the paint booth because they wouldn't crank up. Contrary to what the Caucasians will do. They'll ride around in that two-thousand-dollar car, take that same fifty thousand dollars and put ten thousand dollars into five different properties, rent them out and let the tenants (us) pay the mortgages off. By the time their children are grown up, they will have the properties paid for already.

After getting off the bus, he walks into the probation office. "Hello Mr. Danison," Murk says.

"Let's see ...you failed the drug test two weeks ago, you haven't attempted to register for school to get your G.E.D., you say it's because you're working, but you don't have a job.

Look, all I'm asking from you is to pay your probation fee and stay clean. You're already two months behind in payments and this makes your third month in a row not paying. If you don't pay by next month or start working by your next visit, I'm going to violate you, then back to prison you go," his probation officer told him.

Sitting in a brand new pink Dodge Challenger with twenty-two inch pink Diablous, Monique is waiting in McDonald's drive- through watching Murk come out of the probation office. She's an older woman who has a fetish for young, thugged out men who get money. Not only is she a gold digger, but a nymphomaniac as well. Some men don't mind paying, because she's worth it. She watches Murk walk in McDonalds, so she pulls out of the drive-through lane, parks, and rushes in behind him.

Murk's waiting in line with three dollars and fifty cents left. All he can afford is a ninety-nine cent special quarter pounder with cheese, no fries, no drink, no nothing. He needs at least a dollar and fifty cents to catch the bus back home.

Monique bumps into him and drops her purse. "Excuse me," she says. She bends over slowly, then squats down in her Apple Bottom jeans, with a Nicki Minaj booty, a prep perky breast, with her cleavage showing and nipples sticking out. She tries to balance herself on her high heels while she squats down to pick up her purse. It seemed like the whole McDonalds stopped and froze. The only thing moving was her bending over and squatting down to pick up her purse. Murk is stuck for words. He thought his heart stopped beating when it dropped from the rush of excitement he got when she bumped into him. She has a face and body that would kill, except the type of kill her face has is drop-dead ugly kill! Her body left her face at the bottom of the dime scale. Her face was more like a few pennies - one or two cents, far away from a dime. Murk helped her pick up her purse.

"Thanks, you're such a gentleman, how can I pay you back?" A stranger next to Murk tells him, "Bro, she's digging you. Pay for her food then ask for her number," as Monique is on her way over to the sidebar to get some napkins, twisting her ass from left to right in her high heels. It seemed like each butt cheek had its own step and her booty was walking without any legs, because when she walked, that's all you saw. The guy next to Murk is steadily tapping him like he knows him. He says, "Go on bro. holla at her, be a gentleman and pay for her food."

She walks back. Something took Murk over. The same mood and rush he feels when he gets ready to do something, took him over. This is that same rush of encouragement which ran through him when he robbed that lady for her purse, when he attacked his Stepfather, and when he killed the car dealer.At first he's scared as hell, then all of a sudden, another side takes him over.

"So what's your name lil momma?" asks Murk.

"Monique," she says, smiling. She's looking at Murk's two hundred and fifty dollar jeans, his hundred and fifty-dollar shirt. She scoped him up and down estimating his gear at close to a thousand dollars. She really thinks she's scoring a lick.

"I'm saying momma, I'm sorta in a rush and I would love to chop it up with you and get to know you better. So let me pay for your food, get your number and I'll holla at you later on tonight," he tells her. "May I take your order?" asks the worker.

"Whatever Ms. Monique wants, and a quarter pounder with cheese," said Murk.

"Hold on one minute, let me ask the manager if the quarter pounder with cheese is still on sale," the worker said.

"I want number three," Monique tells her before she leaves the counter. Monique goes into her purse and pulls out a business card and hands it to Murk. It reads, "Monique's Beauty Salon". After Murk reads the business card he looked up and saw the worker coming back to the counter. All of a sudden he came back to reality and realized that he only has three dollars and fifty cents, knowing that Monique's meal is five dollars alone.

"Excuse me, I'll be right back, I got to use the bathroom," said Murk. He rushes to the restroom around the corner. Instead of using the restroom, he hits the side door and takes off running.

CHAPTER SIXTEEN

Coupe calls Kino. "Me and Poochy will be there in five minutes." They pull up to Kino's apartment Murk and Kino come out carrying their fishing rods.

"What we using for bait?" asks Kino.
"We gonna dig up some worms," answered Coupe.

When Kino and his click were younger, they would ride their bicycles all through Pinehills, going from one lake to another fishing. They only had two bicycles between the four of them. Murk and Kino would start off first peddling, gripping the rods and the steering at the same time, towing Coupe and Poochy while they sat on the handlebars carrying the tackle. On the way back home, they would switch. Whoever caught the least fish between each pair would be the one who carries all the fish back. Now that they are old enough to drive and Coupe owns a car, they drive to the lakes.

There's a canal in Pinehills that flows from the lake at Barnett Park. They have to park the car in the neighborhood and cut through the houses to get to the canal. They pull up to the houses. The only thing between them and the canal is a fence to climb, with two Doberman pinchers and a Rottweiler mix. Kino designs the plan as he always does.

"Coupe, you and Murk go on the other side of the house to divert the dog's attention while we jump the fence and make it across. Then we'll draw them to us, that's when yall cross.

Coupe and Murk go to one side of the house. Murk kicks the fence and yells "Aye!" The dogs take off running full speed. One of them head-butts the fence trying to get at them. "Damn, that one's crazy as hell," Murk said. The dogs were showing nothing but teeth and saliva dripping, growling like they haven't eaten in days. Coupe and Murk could be their supper. On the other side of the house Kino and Poochy hop the fence and run across the yard. When they get half way across, one of the man-eaters sees them and takes off towards them. If Poochy and Kino never ran track before in their lives, they should've been track stars that day, because they both hauled ass when they saw the dog coming at them. Poochy damn near hurdled the fence. Kino dropped his rod. They both barely made it across. Poochy and Kino then diverted both of the dog's attention so Murk and Coupe could make it across. Both groups met up.

"Damn, I dropped my rod," Kino said.

"Yall three take the dogs on the other side and I'll get it," Murk volunteered.

When they left to distract the dogs, Murk pulled out the gun he took from the car dealer and placed it on the ground so he could hop the fence and get the fishing rod. As soon as the dogs run to attack Kino and the others, Murk hops the fence to get the rod. For some reason, one of the dogs seems like he knows this trick and he keeps his eye on the other side of the fence. This particular dog sees Murk before he grabs the rod and takes off at him. Murk sees the dog coming. Instead of turning around to head back across the fence, he dashes to the fishing rod, grabs it, throws it over the fence, and takes off running.

When he gets five feet away from the fence, he leaps into the air toward the fence. The dog is ten feet away, takes a couple more steps, then leaps into the air behind Murk. Murk lands on the fence and starts climbing. The mix terror breed lands on Murk with his jaws on Murk's ass. The dog is hanging, holding on to Murk's ass. Murk damn near let go of the fence and fell backward into the yard. The other dog is on his way. Murk grips the fence with one hand then punches the dog in the face with the other hand. After the third blow, the dog lets go while the other dog is now in the air headed at Murk. After the man-eater lets go, Murk clears over the fence just in time. His clothes are ripped up and his booty is scratched up, but he's OK. It would have been a different story if he had fallen back into that yard with both of those dogs there. The boys cross the dam over the canal and go into the woods to dig up some worms, and catch some crickets and grasshoppers to fish with. Then they followed the canal to where it meets the lake.

"There goes a gator," Coupe said.

"There goes another one." Murk takes out his gun and shoots at them.

"What the hell are you doing? They ain't done nothing to you! Put that shit up!" Kino said. Kino gets mad when Murk does stupid unnecessary things. Kino loves peace. He's like 2Pac, "*I'm not a killer, but don't push me.*" Murk, on the other hand, is a killer.

They all bait their hooks then cast their rods.

"My Father started back drinking and beat my Mother up," said Poochy.

"Damn, why he did that?" asked Kino.

"Because we don't have no money and we're about to lose the church and the house."

"We in the same boat, Mom car got repoed. Thanks to Murk, he hit the cash three and paid it off, then spent the rest on our outfits. But next month we'll be in the same predicament."

70

"I'm tired of being broke and not having no money. I want to be able to help Mom for taking me in because I don't have nowhere else to go," said Murk. He calls Mrs. B. Mom because his mother is dead.

'I just want to get my shine on and fuck all the hoes," said Coupe.

"I want to buy Mom a house and move her out the projects," said Kino.

"Me, I got to pay off Grand pop's church mortgage and Mama's house," said Poochy.

"I want to help Mom and buy a house for my sister," said Murk.

"What we going to do because this McDonalds mess ain't working," said Poochy.

"Let's rob McDonalds," said Murk.

"Hell no nigga, you crazy?" said Kino.

"Why not. Fuck them crackers," said Poochy.

"I'm with it," said Coupe.

All three of them at the same time said to Coupe, "Nigga, you ain't gonna do shit," Then they started laughing.

"I got a bite!" Kino's reeling in a fish, then all of a sudden a gator snatches it and pops the line. "Damn I had a big one!"

"I told you, you shoulda let me kill them," Murk said.

The owner of the dogs came home early from work. He feeds his dogs and notices footprints and a torn piece of cloth by the fence. He picks it up...

"I want to be rolling like Giovoni" said Poochy.

"That's what I'm talking about," said Coupe.

"Let's holla at him," said Kino.

"We can buy big nicks from Doeboy and sell them for ten dollars," said Murk.

"That's the lick. When I get paid, I'm uh flip my whole check," said Kino.

"Me too," said Poochy.

"Me three," said Coupe.

Murk is sitting there wondering what money he's going to flip because he has none. No job, no check. Kino is already thinking for Murk.

"Murk, I'll ask Mom for ten dollars and tell her we're going to the movies. We'll buy two nicks with that and start from there." They pack it up and start heading back to the car. They get to the gate. Kino looks at the house and notices that the blinds in one of the rooms are open and the barbecue grill is moved from where it was.

"I think somebody's home now."

"Everybody's still at work," Coupe said.

"Aight, who going first?" Poochy asks.

"We going first this time," Murk said.

These are not normal dumb dogs. These are professionally trained dogs. They wouldn't eat a steak if you tried to feed it to them. They are getting keen to the trick Kino and his click are playing.

Poochy and Kino go to the other side to distract the dogs. Coupe and Murk clear the fence and make it across safe. The owner is on the toilet. He hears the dogs barking and figures it's probably a rabbit, raccoon or opossum. His house is close to woods, so all kinds of animals come in the yard, and his dogs try to eat them. Now it's Coupe and Murk's turn to distract the dogs so Kino and Poochy can cross over. They made the distraction and the dogs ran to them, but this same dog lingers behind. Kino notices it but still goes. They hit the fence and run for the other side.

Just like before with Murk, the dog that lingers behind notices them and turns around and heads toward Kino and Poochy. Poochy takes off like Usain Bolt and Kino is right behind him. They both throw their rods over and take a leap for the fence. Both dogs are at them now. Poochy leaps, hits the fence and makes it over. Soon as Kino's right foot steps to leap, he steps into a pothole, trips and falls. That two-second fall was enough time for the Doberman pincher and half Rottweiler man-eaters to be on his ass. The owner definitely knows this is not a rabbit as he hears a young boy yelling and growls from his dogs. He wipes his ass as fast as he can, gets dressed, grabs his pistol and heads out to the back yard.

Just as fast as the dogs were on Kino, Murk went back over that fence, pulled out his gun, and fired.

"Pop! Pop! Pop! Pop! Pop! Pop! Pop! Pop!" It was decreed by Allah, (God) that Kino didn't get hit. Most of the shots were directly on the dogs, because Kino got up while the dogs laid there. Murk kept shooting until he emptied his clip.

The sliding glass door opens. Murk is out of bullets. A tall dark skinned fair-built man stood there with a Glock in his hand. He looks at his dogs, screams and runs towards them. Kino, Murk, Coupe and Poochy haul ass. The owner rushes to his dogs, grabs them and starts crying saying, "NOOOOO!"

He's enraged with anger and looks to see where Kino and his click are going. They hit the fence and dash to the car. Things get complicated for them when they make it to the car. It's only a two door vehicle and the front seat doesn't slide up. They squeeze in there.

"Hurry up!" they yell at each other.
"He's coming over the fence," Poochy yells.

Coupe cranks the car up. The owner of the dogs clears the gate and runs dead at them, pointing his gun. They take off and he shoots the back window out. The owner of the dogs calls the police. The detective retrieves all the bullet shells and gets a description of the car and the suspects.

CHAPTER SEVENTEEN

"Mom?"

"What?"

"You got ten dollars to spare? Me and Murk are going to the movies. I have money to pay for the movies. We just want a few dollars to buy something to eat."

She started to tell them hell no, I don't have any money to spare. But she looked at Kino's stitches all over his body from the dog bites and felt pity for him. She missed her husband and was sad that Kino grew up with his Father being locked up all his life. She also thought about Murk's situation with his Mother dead and Father locked up for life.

"Look in my purse on the counter."

Kino looks in her purse and sees two, five dollar bills, wondering if this is her last ten dollars. He knows she doesn't have any credit cards and doesn't get paid for another week. He takes the money. He and Murk walk across the street to the Palms Apartments.

It's like a whole other city inside these apartments. There's one way in and one way out. Each breezeway has something for sale. In the fifth breezeway you have Ms. Candis, the candy lady. She sells flips, frozen Kool-Aid in a plastic cup, pickled eggs, candy, drinks, homemade cookies, pies and cakes. In the ninth breezeway sits old Paul, who sells bootleg liquor, homemade moonshine, beer and cigarettes after hours. In the same breezeway across the hall is Mango, who sells cocaine powder to the snorters. The last breezeway on the right is Doeboy who hustles all the big nicks, big dimes, eight balls and fifty packs of crack. In the third breezeway, Dolly sells weight in powder - ounces, eighths, quarters, and halves. He gets the blocks from Giovoni. Good-head Jean is in the first breezeway, who boosts and sells all the children's clothes. So many basers come through trading any and every thing for crack. All Wal-Mart products are available in the Palms. You can get a fresh cut from Jay. Jacky does all the pinch plaits, braids and dreads. Chaz in the back has the weed - kush, purple haze or regular. Whatever you want. Fee-Fee has women for sale. Exotic dates, with head and pussy included. You got to have big money though. All her chicks are dimes and they're not messing with no scrubs. Mama Duke has fried fish and fries on Friday. Dinners on the weekends include oxtails, fried chicken, collard greens and cornbread - all soul food. Everybody hanging out on the block has dope and compete for the dope fiend's business.

By the time Kino and Murk get to the second breezeway, they see a fight break out. It's two hoodrats going at it, swinging like men on each other, and no one is breaking it up.

"Ain't that her brother running to the bushes, pulling out that Gat?" asked Kino.

"That's because the girl she's fighting's boyfriend is standing there with his hand in his pants like he's getting ready to pull his fire," replied Murk.

"Look at these jits, Murk. Ain't that Dereck and Pete?"

"Yeah, they in Charley's car."

"Who's Charley?"

"Charley that big money cracker who rents his car out for dope," replied Murk.

These jits can't even drive, riding all fast through the parking lot. Giovoni steps out from Fee-Fee's apartment.

"Get them jits before they make the block hot!" Giovoni yells to the thugs on the block.

"They say he fucking Fee-Fee and that's why nobody can't buy that pussy," Murk told Coupe.

Dragging one foot as he walks along, dirty jeans, mangled hair, jaws moving up and down, side to side, twitching, with a balled up ten-dollar bill in his hand, runs up to Murk.

"Let me get a dime."

Before you know it, five dudes run up to the baser and spit a bunch of rocks out of their mouths into their hands. They all compete to make the sale.

Murk asks one of them, "Where Doeboy at?"
"He's in the back, the last breezeway."
Kino and Murk walk to the back of the Palms.
"What's up Doeboy?"
"What's up Murk?"
"How's that Gat I got ya?"
"Good."
"What's up? What you need?"
"This is my brother, Kino.   You know we stay across the street in Peppertree."
"Yeah, I be seeing yall to the store and around."
Kino gives him some dap and says, "What's up bro? We need two big nicks."
"Come on," he tells Kino.

They follow him as he walks in the breezeway into an apartment. They're in the kitchen and Doeboy goes to the cabinet and pulls out a shoebox. Kino's eyes get big as he sees four bags of cut up dope. One bag is full of eight balls, another is filled with fifty- packs, the third bag has all dimes. He pulls out the fourth bag that has all the big nicks, opens it up, and grabs a handful of them and places them on the table.

"Pick you two of them," he says.

Kino grabs the two biggest nicks and gives ten dollars to Doeboy.

"I'll holla at ya bro," Kino and Murk say as they walk out of the apartment.

"I'll be here in the back," Doeboy yells to them.

They're walking back toward the front and Murk says, "We're gonna sell these two nicks for ten dollars each."

Before they could reach the next breezeway, a fiend stops them.

"I got fifty dollars."

Kino pulls out the two nicks and sees three hustlers running towards him. Kino thinks quick. He snatches the fifty dollars out of the fiend's hand then gives him the two nicks. He tells him, "I'll be right back." One of the three hustlers running towards them yells out, "Aye! That's my jug!"

Kino has the fifty dollars and has left to go see Doeboy, leaving Murk and the jug left standing there.

"What the hell you doing?   Where the twenty dollars you owe me? I know you ain't spending my money with this nigga," said one of the hustlers to the jug.

"I, I, I, I, I, didn't see you," he replied, stuttering.

"You know where I'm at. Your ass think you slick, spending my money with the next man.

He looks at Murk and asks him, "How much he spent with you?"

"He didn't spend nothing with me."

Kino walks up with four big dimes and two nicks. He gives the jug one big dime and one nick, leaving Kino with seventy dollars' worth of dope.

"What the hell," yelled the hustler. He swung on the jug and knocked him to the ground and took all the dope he had.

"I only owe you twenty, that dime is mines," the jug said while on the ground.

"Fuck you. I'm going to teach you about spending my money with the next man."

Murk is eyeing him the whole time, waiting for him to say

anything slick to Kino or himself, so he can get in his ass. He felt Murk's seriousness and never looked Murk's way nor said anything to Murk or Kino. He cussed the jug out then walked away.

"I was waiting for that nigga to say something so I coulda knocked his ass out."

Kino helps the baser fiend up and says, "Bump him, we trying to get this money." He turns to the jug. "You aight?"

"Hell no, he took my dope."

"Here goes a dime, just holla at me when you get straight," Kino told the jug, trying to build a clientele.

"What, what you doing bro?" Murk asks Kino.

"Just chill Murk, I got this."

Kino tells the jug as he walks away," I'm Kino," then looks at Murk and tells him, "We got three big dimes left, that's sixty dollars. We started with ten dollars, and now we got a customer."

They flipped that dope four times, took some losses, and ended up with three hundred dollars. When they came home that night, Kino put fifty dollars in his Mother's purse when she wasn't looking. The next day Poochy and Coupe came over and Kino told them everything that happened. They all planned to walk across the street to the Palms and holla at Doeboy and start flipping that work.

Coupe brags about the two hundred dollars he has to spend, and how he's going to make a million dollars. Kino pulls out the two hundred and fifty dollars he and Murk made yesterday.

"I don't have no money, I haven't got paid yet," said Poochy.

Kino gives Poochy fifty dollars to buy his own dope. Then he gives Murk a hundred, leaving him a hundred to himself. They walk across the street to the Palms Apartments and heads to the back to find Doeboy. Everyone except Murk spends all their money. He only spends fifty dollars out of his hundred. He goes to Chaz in the sixth breezeway and buys some weed. Then he makes his way to old man Paul to buy some blunts and beer. He kept the rest of the money for some wings and fries from Lee's store later on after he smokes the weed.

Walking through the Palms, there are niggas everywhere hanging out. They get some dirty looks from people who are wondering about Poochy and Coupe. Murk rolls up the weed and everybody starts smoking and drinking, except Kino. He's about that money. They start serving and everybody sells out two or three times. Coupe ends up with seven hundred dollars, Murk ends up with four hundred, Poochy ends up with five hundred and Kino ends up with only three hundred dollars. But, Kino was making deals and locking in customers, accumulating more clout than everybody else that will pay off for him later. They all give Coupe fifty dollars apiece so he can get his car out of the shop. The back window was being replaced after being shot out by the owner of the dogs Murk killed.

The next day Coupe goes to Men's Closet and puts four hundred dollars down on an eight-hundred-dollar outfit. Poochy give all his money to his mother, except a hundred dollars. His Mother kisses him and tells him thanks. Poochy's little sister LaQuita asks her Mother, "Mama, can I please go on the field trip with my class, pleeeaaassseee?"

"I have to pay bills LaQuita."

"It's only thirty dollars."

Poochy reaches in his pocket. "Here you go," and gives his sister thirty dollars.

"Thank you big brother," as she jumps into his arms and hugs him.

Murk bought more weed and beer and gave Mrs. Betterman a hundred dollars. Kino didn't spend a dime. He invested every penny he had back into the game.

The next day Kino skipped school and went on the block early in the morning. All of the overnight hustlers who were up all night were taking it in. It's 7:00 a.m.Hardly anyone is on the block, money is coming slowly. Kino leans with his back against the wall, right foot up on the wall protruding his right knee out. A big body Benz S550 pulls in the breezeway. The passenger side tinted window comes down.

A slim older White chick with smeared make up, looking like she's been up for a few days, asks Kino if he had a hundred. Kino is spooked. He wants the hundred-dollar sale. The Benz is what scares him. He tells her to get out and walk around the corner with him. He wants to do the serve out of the eyes of whoever's driving that vehicle. They walk inside the breezeway and disappear out of the driver's sight. Looking at this older woman, weighing a hundred and five pounds soaking wet, dressed like a prostitute with two days' worth of old makeup on, Kino knows for sure she's smoking crack.

Kino asks her, "Who is that with you?"

"He owns the Popeye's chicken on Colonial Drive."

"He smokes?"

"Like a chimney. He only wants this small amount to test the quality. If it's good, he'll spend at least a thousand before the day's over with."

Kino gives her the dope and his number and tells her to call him before she comes and he'll meet her across the street. Kino is trying to keep this customer to himself, away from the Palms.

At 6:00 p.m. that day they all met in the fifth breezeway of the Palms Apartments.

"Why you ain't come to school Kino?" asked Poochy.

"I'm trying to get this paper and school ain't making me no dollars."

Unfortunately, this is a false ideology that Iblis, the devil, whispers to our minds to lead us astray. Education is the basis of knowledge. Before you can advance in anything, you have to have the basics down pat. We want the whole pie without working or waiting for it. I know dope boys who can't count. How in the world are you going to sell anything and you can't even count? The more educated you are, the more on top of your game you will be, whether it's selling dope, working a 9 to 5, or running your own business. This is because decision making and problem-solving skills develop from education. The best education is that of your Creator. To learn the truth, believe in the truth, act upon the truth, teach the truth, and to bear it with patience and perseverance until Allah Ta'Ala, God The Most High, rescues you.

"You talking about me Poochy, why you ain't at work?" asks Kino. Poochy jabbers back, answering a question with a question.

"Why you ain't at work?"

"Fuck McDonalds, this why I ain't at work nor school."

Kino shows them over a thousand dollars he made all in one day since that morning from skipping school. They all walk to the back to holla at Doeboy. Murk, Poochy and Coupe get their dope. Doeboy looks at Kino.

"What's up Kino?" he asks.

Kino waits for his boys to walk out, then he tells Doeboy, "I got a thousand dollars, I don't want no big dimes. You got some cookies?"

"You gotta holla at T for that, but I got ten eight balls for ya."

"Nah bro, I'll holla at ya."

Kino leaves and goes to the second breezeway. "What's up T?" asks Kino.

"What's up Kino?"

"What a cookie going for?"

"I was wondering when you was going to stop petty

hustling and holla at me. "

"I'm trying to move up, not down," replied Kino.

They go inside to the kitchen and T shows Kino a key of cocaine cooked up in all cookies.

"Four fifty a piece," said T.

"Let me get two of them."

Kino puts them in his pocket and walks across the street to go home and cut it up in all twenties. When he gets home he kisses his Mother and says, "Hey Mom," then gives her the hundred dollars he had left. By the time he made it across the street, the two cookies were already broken down to crumbs. He goes into his room, gets the razor blade he just bought, then puts the dope on his dresser. Looking at the dope, he's puzzled and doesn't know what to do. His phone rings, it's the trick in the Benz.

"What's up?" Kino answers.

"Let me get two hundred. "

"Same spot."

"I'm five minutes away."

"Aight, I'll be there."

There's a Black BMW 740 pulling in. Kino starts to walk away then the window comes down and a person yells, "Kino!" It's that trick who was coming in the Benz. They park and she gets out.

"How many cars he got?" Kino asks.

"That's not him, this another one of my customer. He'll spin a thousand or two if this is the same dope. That yellow you had was that Hard Bernard. This looks too white and chalky. Is it soft?"

"You know how I rock. I keep that iron," Kino replied. He sells it to her then goes back into his house.

Back in The Palms, Coupe, Murk and Poochy are on the

block grinding. Poochy has already flipped his money a couple times.

"There goes Big Money Charley!" Five niggas run up to the car. They're elbow wrestling with each other. The first one to get their arm through the window to show the basers the dope is the one to make the sale. There are about ten to fifteen niggas in this one breezeway. Another car pulls up and Dirty Red beats everybody to the car and snatches the money from the jug and runs. His homeboys don't even know why Dirty Red pulled this stunt. They started to act stupid right along with him. One of them throws a bottle at the windshield and the other punches the jug through the window.

The jug pulls off burning rubber and hits Fee-Fee's car. Everybody went crazy then and started pelting the car with sticks, bricks, rocks, bottles, or whatever the jits could find. The jug spun off and left. Dirty Red came back laughing after the car spun off. Poochy looked at him and said, "Why you did that?"

"Cause I wanted to fuck nigga!"

"You messing up the money. It's niggas like you who make million dollar holes hot and the money go away. Last week they said you was selling perk," Poochy told him.

"What you going to do about it, fuck-nigga?"

Poochy swung on his ass, he ducked and swung back. They were trading blows like a boxing match. No grabbing, no wrestling, just swinging Poochy catches him with a wild left hook and staggers Dirty Red. That's when Red's homeboy runs at Poochy, but Murk caught his ass with a mean right hook that knocked his ass out. Before you know it, there was two more niggas on Poochy and two more on Murk. Coupe must have grown some balls because this time he picked up a stick and started swatting them niggas in the head, back, or wherever he could connect. Now there are about a hundred niggas out. No one else jumps in, they just watch.

"Pop! Pop! Pop! Pop!" It's Fee-Fee shooting in the air, and the fight breaks up.

"I told yall about that crazy mess in my breezeway. If Giovoni comes around, all yall niggas dead," Fee-Fee screamed with the pistol in her hand.

Murk, Poochy, and Coupe walk back across the street to tell Kino. They walk in the house.

"What happen to yall?" Kino asks.
"Dirty Red with that bullshit," Poochy said.

Kino's phone rings. It's the trick in the BMW.

"What's up?" Kino says as he answered the phone.

"That's some bullshit water-down dope you sold me. Just wanted to tell you." Then she hung up the phone.

"Murk, where you going?" asked Kino.

"Them niggas got me fucked up." He grabs his pistol then slams the door on his way out.

"Come on yall," Kino tells Poochy and Coupe.

They all fall behind Murk, then Kino tells them, "If we are going to do this nigga, let's do it for good reason. We ain't trying to go to prison, and be where our father's at. Let's be smart, so chill out. We'll get this nigga when the time is right, and for the right reason."

Murk thought about Kino's words, calmed down, and followed him.

"Come on, I got to go holla at T," said Kino.

Doeboy buys cookies from T and breaks them down to balls, big dimes, big nicks and fifty packs, and has a few power jugs for himself.

T buys powder from Dolly and cooks up the cookies. And Dolly buys the blocks from Giovoni.

"What's up T?" Kino asked.

"You ready for some more?" asks T.

"Nah. That was some water you sold me, it broke all up. It was no good."

"It was dope; I don't know what the fuck you talking about."

"I'm not saying you perk me, I'm saying you sold me some whip, some bullshit water and I'm losing customers. "

"Once you walk out that door, the dope is yours."

Murk pulls out his fire, puts one in the chamber and says,

"So what you saying fuck-nigga, you going to straighten my brother, or what?"

Murk was not pointing the gun at him, just letting T know that he's strap.

Next thing you know, four niggas who were down with T pull out guns and tell Murk, "What's up jit, you don't want none of this?" Murk doesn't care anything about his life. He's about to go for what he knows when all of a sudden Giovoni comes around the corner and yells, "What the fuck going on?"

T and his boys put their guns down because they know what type of time Giovoni's on and he is not with unnecessary violence, especially in his trap. The whole Palms Apartments is his trap. He made it, he supplied it, weed and all.

"Jit, put that gun up!" Giovoni told Murk.

Murk always respected Giovoni for some reason. So he put it up.

Giovoni told T and his goons to fall back and he'll holla at them later. Then he turned to Kino and his click and said, "Let me holla at yall."

Fee-Fee called Giovoni and told him what happened to her car and what she had heard about, why Poochy went off on Dirty Red and the big fight behind that.

"Let me spit some real shit to yall. I've been watching you and Kino for a minute. Real niggas sense real niggas. I see the loyalty you have Murk. You seem like you're loyal to whoever's down with you. You won't cross them and you'll die for them. The key to your success is being like that for the right person, and not the wrong one. A good heart person who loves you the same. A person who will keep you out of trouble when you listen to him. One who will always have your back when no one else will. If you keep it real with anyone else less than that, they will leave you hanging and will let you destroy yourself."

All Murk could think about was Kino, how he shared his room, his Mother, his food, and his home with him. Whenever they went anywhere, Kino was always the one who either paid for Murk' s way and bought his food, or he didn't do it for either Murk or himself. They did it together or they didn't do it at all. And he always talked Murk out of doing something stupid that would've destroyed him. Giovoni turns to Kino and says, "As for you Kino, I see myself in you all day. You the brains of this click. You have a good heart, but others will take the good in you for one who is weak. This is not to say that you are weak, but to say you will be tried over and over again. Each time you will prove that you're not weak, but will find yourself being tried again.

To save yourself a lot of hassle, you need to surround yourself with strength. Basically a maniac, so people would know that it will be a repercussion for trying you. Prevention leads to less drama. The best way to prevent unnecessary drama is with fear, and the good guy doesn't put fear in people, a maniac does. Just think, no matter how many people you kill, if you be nice to the next man, he'll think he can get over on you. But take a maniac, for instance, he doesn't have to kill nobody, but the next person will always think twice about trying this maniac. So keep a couple of them down with you. I know you will love them and treat them right, because that's just you. And they will love and kill for you. To win in this game, you need muscle and brains.

If you roll with that combination, everything else will come."

Giovoni didn't tell Kino about the snitches, prison, death, and the destruction that drugs do to the families of both the seller and user. In the streets, we never realize or think about the negative consequences of the dope game until it's too late. Too late would be sitting in a prison cell with a lot of time, telling God, "I would STOP if I had ONE LAST CHANCE. Too late would be after your wife, your Mother, your kids, or someone else in your family gets kidnapped, tied up and tortured, held for ransom as a hostage, waiting for you to come home. Too late would be when your six feet under, pushing up daisies.

What needs to be told to our young men in the streets is what Anas bin Malik, may Allah be pleased with him, reported Muhammad, peace and blessings be upon him, to have said. *"When carried to his grave, a dead person is followed by three, two of which return, and one remains with him. His relatives, his property and his deeds follow him. His relatives and his property return back while his deeds remain with him."*

With that being said, all the sins from the dope game only accumulated bad deeds that you will be recompensed for when you are resurrected. All the money, women, property you made returns back, but every sinful act you accumulated from the streets will stay with you. Your deeds, good and bad.

While Giovoni is talking to Poochy and Coupe, Kino sees the trick in that BMW riding into the breezeway. Ten niggas take off running at the car.

"Damn, she didn't even call me," Kino thought. This time she brought another prostitute who has a big money customer as well. So both of them spent money. Two of the dudes come back from the car, walking by Kino.

"Man, she spent two hundred," one of them said.

"The trick in the back seat spent two hundred too," the other one replied.

Kino tells Giovoni what happened between him and T. Giovoni tells Kino to bring the dope back to Fee-Fee's house. Then he goes and hollas at T and says, "Bring me two bowls to Fee-Fee's house and keep unnecessary drama away from my money." Kino goes across the street to get the dope and heads back to Fee-Fee' s house. Murk, Coupe and Poochy head to Doeboy to re-up and get back on the block. Kino is at Fee-Fee's front door. (knock, knock)

A sexy female voice from behind the door asks, "Who is it?"

"Kino," he replies. A voice sounds like he's screaming from far away.

"Let him in," Giovoni told the high-class hoodrat. Kino walks in hearing Trick Daddy and C-lo playing "*I'm a oh sneaky oh freaky oh geechie ass nigga, collard green neck bone eatin' ass nigga.*" He sees three girls in G-strings, no bras, drinking and dancing with each other. They're rolling on Megatrons. Giovoni walks to the kitchen and tells Kino, "Give me the dope." He turns on the stove, grabs the bowl, puts water in it, grabs the baking soda, then divides the crushed up dope in half.

"Damn, you crushed this dope up," said Giovoni.

"That water, it broke soon as I put it in my pocket. I felt it breaking. I was gonna cut it all up in twenties anyway, so I didn't mind it breaking, but when I took it out and it was all mushed up, I had to bring it back to him."

"You can't put no water in your pocket. You got to babysit that kind of dope and get up off it in weight or re-cook it. You got to know your dope, know who you buy from. See Doeboy only buys Iron. T will sell Iron cookies and water cookies. A lot of them jits on the block just hustle. They don't see it as a business. They want big dope and a quick flip, grinding out everything. They have no pride in their work, they'll sell whatever and to whoever. Don't be like that. Pick your customers, keep that Iron and customers will pick you.

There's some power jugs who you would never imagine smoke crack. A lot of them cater to tricks. They smoke and trick. Some will never take a step in these projects, you have to go to them. Get them power jugs on your team, then you will save yourself a lot of problems and make a lot of money. You have to keep that Iron, that Hard Bernard and treat them like a business, and they will never leave you."

Giovoni drops the dope in a white Pyrex bowl with a handle that was purchased from Wal-Mart. These special type of bowls are made to be placed directly on the stove without cracking or breaking. Kino watches as Giovoni places the dope and baking soda in the bowl. He lets the little bit of water come to a boil. As the dope starts popping, he takes a fork and whips it while it's frying, making the dope bigger. This is called frying the dope. Now the dope is floating on top of the water, so he takes the bowl to the sink, turns on the water and sprinkles water on top of the dope until it all falls down into one large gel at the bottom of the bowl. He then takes some dish detergent and pours a couple of drops on the gel, puts the bowl down and watches it spread like a pancake.

"Kino, the trick to having Iron when you cook is letting it dry under the water. Sometimes it takes longer to dry, but you have that Iron. If I was to whip this dope and make it eat the rest of that water, it will dry fast and blow up and fill that whole bowl, but you'll have water then." He places the bowl on the counter then says, "It's been so long ago since I cooked in this kitchen, I forgot these kitchen countertops are all unlevel. I got to put this on the floor. If I let it dry on this unlevel countertop, you'll have a warped sided cookie. I fried this cookie and blowed the gel up, but I let it dry underwater. I didn't whip it causing it to blow up by making that gel eat the water. So it's way better quality than what you initially bought. But it's not that Iron which is how I'm going to drop this second cookie."

Giovoni grabbed the second bowl and put a little more water than he did for the first bowl. He did the same process, except he didn't fry the dope and he let it boil a little longer. When he got ready to take it off the stove, he told Kino to grab two pieces of paper from off the table and fold them together in half, then fold it again.

After he had sprinkled water on top to drop all the floating dope down to one gel, he said, "I forgot the trick I used to do when I was coming up back in the days before your time. I had this whole floor filled with bowls. I had no more room. I needed to use the counter tops.

"What you use to do?" asked Kino.

"Hand me that paper I told you to fold." Kino handed it to him and he placed it on the low side of the bowl making it now higher than the other side. He took the paper back from under the bowl and unfolded one-half of it, then placed the paper back under the lower side and said, "Perfect, it's leveled out. Now, this is that Hard Bernard, that Iron. It's not as big as the first cookie, but you'll have the jugs walking by all the other niggas looking for you."

"I got to use this to get my trick back, the one who pulled up in that BMW when you was talking to Poochy and Coupe," said Kino.

"I saw you looking at that car and mumbling something," said Giovoni.

"I thought you was talking to Poochy and Coupe when that power jug in the BMW came through," Kino said.

"I was, but in this game, you have to be aware of everything. Let me tell you what to do. When you're on the block, serve this cookie." He pointed to the first one he cooked and said, "It's better than the whipped dope you bought from T, but not as good as the Iron from Doeboy. All them jugs coming with seven dollars for a dime, wanting two-for-one deals, wanting you to front them, give them this dope. But this Iron over here," he pointed to the bowl on the counter, "serve this to your power jugs, your main loyal customers. This is how you keep them in your pocket," Giovoni explained.

He got something to drink out of the refrigerator and

offered Kino some, but he declined. Giovoni continued, "Some dope dries on the fork while you're spreading it, some takes longer to dry, like five, ten or fifteen minutes. You also have the dope we call HBO, meaning, you better go watch a movie on HBO while you're waiting for it to dry. I even had dope, where I went to sleep and woke up in the morning to pull it out of the bowls."

Giovoni is testing Kino, seeing where he's at, and teaching him at the same time. "You smoke?" Giovoni asking another test question.

"No," replied Kino.

"You pop pills. Tiesha got what you want," Giovoni says as he leads Kino into the living room where Tiesha is eating another girl's pussy while a third girl is fucking Tiesha with a strap on.

Giovoni calls Fee-Fee, winks at the three girls, and points his head at Kino, then walks into the room with Fee-Fee. The one who was fucking Tiesha comes straight to Kino and starts unzipping his pants. Kino's dick is rock hard, ready to jump out at her. As soon as she starts sucking and deep throating him, Tiesha stops eating the girl's pussy and jumps on Kino. Now he has two fine ass women sucking the hell out of him. He looks at the girl who was getting her pussy ate. She's laying on her back with her legs in the air, playing with her pussy. She takes the dildo that Tiesha was getting fucked with and starts sliding it inside her while she's rubbing her clitoris with the other hand. As soon as Kino saw that dildo go inside her, he thought about his dick going inside her. Then she started making noise breathing loud. Kino's plan was to fuck all three of them, but it was too much excitement for his first threesome, and he nutted as soon as she started making noises when she put the dildo in her. He nutted all on both of the girl's faces who were sucking his dick.

They started kissing each other and Kino laid back and

said, "Damn, I didn't even fuck."

Giovoni walked out and said, "Damn, that was quick," and laughed.

"Let's check this dope," he told Kino. He picked up the bowl and wiggled it and saw the whole cookie slide. He knew then it was ready to come out. Giovoni looks at Kino and says, "Go clean yourself up, your dope ready."

Fee-Fee comes out, looks at Kino and laughs, then says, "Next time yall go in the room with that."

Kino washes up in the bathroom, comes back out and says to Giovoni, "So if I put these cookies in my pocket, they not gonna break?"

"Yeah, they gonna break, but they won't be crumbs and all smooshed up. They will be in pieces. You got to cut it up."

"You got a razor blade?" Kino asked.

"Give'em here" Giovoni told Kino.

Giovoni is a pro at all stages of this game, from the bottom to the top. He takes the cookie and uses his fingernail to draw a line down the middle of it, then pops it in half. Then he takes one of the halves, and using his fingernail slices it up into five eight balls, then he pops each one individually.

He tells Kino, "Cut them all up in balls, put them in a bag, then you'll be OK."

Kino is looking at him and saying to himself, "Damn he's smart!" Kino thanks him then leaves out to go back to his house. He walks through the breezeway into the parking lot and see four niggas rushing a jug spitting dope out their mouths into their hands to serve him.

"I don't see how they put that cocaine in their mouths," Kino tells one of the hustlers posted up.

"Most of them niggas snort cane anyway, so putting it in their mouths ain't nothing to them," he told Kino.

"What you said they call that?" Kino asks.

"Gumlining."

"Man, I seen Mae-Mae cut up a whole eight ball and put it

in his mouth."

"Yeah bro, you just push it deep down in your gums all around your teeth. It has your mouth numb as hell."

"What's the purpose?" Kino asks.

"So them crackers won't get it off you."

****

Gumlining has its advantages and disadvantages that could be fatal. One advantage is when the jump-out police attack you, you can run without them seeing you throw down the dope. When they see you throw down the dope, the authorities go back and retrieve the drugs you threw down, then charge you for it. Those who throw down their drugs and get away usually end up losing that dope. Either the police get it, somebody watching you being chased comes and gets it, or you go back to retrieve it, and you probably won't find it. But if you run with the dope in your mouth and don't have to swallow it, you get away and still have your dope. By gumlining you also avoid being caught unexpectedly by undercover police popping out of nowhere surprising you, and catching you with dope in your pocket.

Another advantage is that hustlers who bag up the nicks and dimes individually will have a more severe charge resulting in a higher bond and more jail time, versus the dope being in your mouth minus the bags. Whenever the dope is bagged up the charge is possession with intent to distribute. You can have the same amount of drugs without a bag, then the charge will be simple possession, unless it's a large amount. Competition is steep on the block. One jug comes for dope and there could be up to ten niggas rushing him at the same time. First one with the dope usually gets the serve. While the competition is going into their pockets and pulling it out of bags, or running to their stash spot in the bushes, the gumliner is there, spits the dope out of his mouth into his hand and in seconds the dope is on display for sale. The serve is complete before the other person even gets his dope out. Those are the advantages of gumlining.

One possible and sometimes fatal disadvantage is swallowing the dope can cause death. I personally know people who died from swallowing dope. The second disadvantage is that there is a slim chance that if the police want you bad enough, they'll take you to the hospital and pump your stomach. It doesn't happen too often, but it does happen. The third disadvantage is dealing with being choked by a muscle-bound police officer with a license to kill. This is part of the street life in Orlando, Florida.

****

Someone yells, "Duke Boys!"

Kino looks and sees two vans and two unmarked cars mobbed out riding fast as hell towards them. Everybody takes off running. They jump out of the van, some dressed in army fatigues others in all black - black gear, black boots, black ski masks, all armed with Glock 40's. But this is not a robbery. The only color you see is their shiny blue eyes piercing through the black ski masks. There's more of them coming around the corner chasing two jitterbugs, Derick and Pete. The foot chase for Pete was too easy. They didn't have a chance. It looked like the rabbit versus the turtle. They couldn't catch him. But you wouldn't be able to say the same for his brother Derick. He was too high on cloud nine. He'd been smoking weed all day. They grabbed Derick and went straight for his neck, choking him trying to prevent him from swallowing the dope. The bear claw grip that's around his throat causes him to spit it up. All you see is niggas running everywhere. Doors are being locked, because if a person runs up in your apartment, the police are coming in after them.

Now the Duke Boys are all in your house. They'll lie and

tell the judge that they smelled weed or saw drugs in plain view which gave them probable cause to search the house. And upon that search they found guns and dope. A nigga might not even know you and he's running up in your house if your door is unlocked. Now you're hit on a humbug.

Kino gets away and sees them chasing Poochy. He's wondering what happened to Murk and Coupe. Poochy turns back into a track star and leaves dust in the eyes of the muscle-bound Duke Boy who was chasing him. The only problem was that there were too many of them coming from different directions. As he outran one, he ran into another one. They cornered him off and attacked him. The big tall cracker grabbed Poochy and slammed him. Another one jumped in the air and landed on Poochy with his knee on his back. They grabbed and twisted his arm, damn near breaking it.

Three officers subdued him. One with his knee and all his weight on Poochy's back, the other one's knee and all his weight on his head, smooshing his face into the ground, while the third one is twisting his arms back to place handcuffs on his wrist. They went back and retrieved the dope he threw down and they pulled more dope out of his pocket. Nobody taught Poochy the gumlining game. They threw Poochy in the back of the van with some more people. Then they rode to Crosstown and pull into the Popeye's on Washington Street and the Trail. They send a decoy on Polk Street to buy a twenty piece. As soon as the dope boy serves the decoy, they let him walk around like everything is good, then they rush him when he least expects them to. They throw him in the van and ride to the next hood. They hit more hoods while Poochy sits in the van handcuffed the whole time. They ride from hood to hood until they fill the van up with arrestees. They stop in Beirut and Poochy notices that two of the dudes put in the van were with the boys he fought in the club over Kino's girl Tanisha. They were so drunk and high that night they don't even remember Poochy. Nobody knew Kino and them, they were jits and nobodies.

One of them said, "You think Dae'Quan going to bail us out?" "If you still owe him from the last bomb then you messed up."

" "Yeah, I do."

"Well, I'm straight, but you might be out of gas."

They took Poochy and Derick to the Juvenile Detention Center.

Both Derick's Mother and Father were strung out on crack. So he had to wait on his Grandmother to come and get him.

Mrs. Mabel came and got Poochy. The drive home was silent. Poochy's face is sore, his back is sore, and his wrists are sore.

They walk into the house and Poochy's mother couldn't take it anymore.

"Why are you working for the devil, Poochy? I raised you better than that."

"Mom, we need the money. Dad left us and Grandpop is too old to work. You take care of us, the church and all the people in the community, so you don't have time to work. Besides, if you did, where would you work?"

Poochy's Mother is a good old, sweet, southern Christian girl, with no education. But, she can cook, clean and take care of her man and her children. She's sweet to everybody in the community. She's the perfect homemaker and charity worker. Everybody in Apopka loves her. But she has no certified skills or education to get a decent job. Poochy thought, "If she works, who would take care of Grandpop, his sister, the church and all the people in the community?"

Poochy tells his Mother in a demanding voice, "McDonalds is not cutting it."

Her eyes begin to water as her voice cracks with cries when she gets louder. "I can't lose you Poochy!" she sobs and grabs him, shaking him. "The streets took both of my brothers, one in prison, the other dead. Your father was next, until we started praying and he left the streets alone." Mrs. Mabel grabs Poochy and turns into a hug, squeezing him as if this was their last hug.

"I love you Poochy."
"I love you too Mommy!"
 Poochy's little sister comes running and crying, saying "Mommy!"
"Come here baby," Mrs. Mabel tells her. They stand in a group hug all together crying and holding each other, each saying "I love you" to the other.
"Let's pray," Mrs. Mabel says. They hold hands, facing each other, tears come out of Poochy's eyes from seeing his Mother in this state, because of his own wrongdoing, that crushes his heart. If there's one person who can get to a man's heart, it's definitely his Mother. No one wants to see their Mother crying because she's worried about them.

When that federal judge announced my sentence, "Two hundred and forty months," a loud cry came out. The courtroom was in silence. I knew that cry, but I still looked around. It was my Mother, wailing with tears coming down her face. Every time I hear Plies' song, "Running my momma crazy," or his other song where he says "Pussy-ass cracker give a nigga a hundred years - have your momma leaving out the courtroom in tears," all I can think about is that moment in that courtroom. Anybody who received a long sentence or is doing time feels what I'm saying.

As they're holding hands in a circle, with their eyes closed, a deep voice comes from far away...
"Hold up, let me get some of this love and praying."
"Grandpop!" LaQuita screams.

He joins hands and Mrs. Mabel says, "Dear Lord, please keep the devil away from Poochy and bring my husband and their Father back home to us safely. Provide for us and protect us from evil. Amen."

"Amen," Poochy, LaQuita and Grandpop said. Poochy hugged his Mother and said, "I'm sorry Mom. Don't worry," and walks to his room. This confused young man lays on the bed and thinks to himself, "We been praying to Jesus all my life and we still struggling and broke." Poochy started comparing in his mind how he bust his ass at McDonalds all week, catching the bus to work and home for only a couple hundred dollars. Then after taxes hit him, he's left with a little over a hundred dollars, versus going on the block and making four to five hundred dollars in one day. He started thinking, "Maybe I could just make enough money to catch Mom up on the house and church mortgage, buy a car, then get out the game."

Little does Poochy know that believing once you start selling dope you can easily stop - is the biggest lie. Selling drugs is just as addicting as smoking crack. How many of us have witnessed that? How many times have we said, *"I'm going to stop when I get ten thousand dollars"*? You make that, now it's fifty thousand, then a hundred. It doesn't stop there, it goes on and on. Each time you accomplish your goal, your stop point, you come up with three more. It never stops, your eyes just get bigger.

Paraphrasing a Qudsi Hadith, Allah's messenger, peace and blessing be upon him, that Allah Ta'Ala, God The Most High, said: *"That if the children of Adam had a valley full of gold, they would desire another one."*

CHAPTER EIGHTEEN

Coupe, Murk, and Kino make it back to Pepper Tree. Kino tells them, "I think they got Poochy."

"They almost got me," Murk said.

"I dropped all my dope," said Coupe.

"I threw all mines down too. Giovoni just got through re-cooking it for me," yelled Kino.

Coupe ends up leaving and going home. Murk went right back out to see if the Duke Boys left. He's ready to go back on the block. Kino takes a long hot shower, fixes him something to eat, then lays on his bed and thinks about his father. He's wondering what's going to happen to Poochy, thinking that could've been him put in the Duke Boys' van. He looks on the nightstand and sees his Father's letter. He picks it up, opens it, and reads it.

Dear Kino,

I know I made a promise to you that I didn't keep. I want you to know that your Father is real as they come, and never would I be fake. I will tell you the truth, and don't expect nothing less than the truth when it's coming from one who is real. Anything less will be uncivilized. I want you to know that I don't regret what I did and if I was free and someone tries you, your Mother or my Mother, I will do the same all over again. That's one thing I don't play about, my family! You have my blood and I'm sure you'll kill for your Mother and soon to be wife and children as well. Kino, I LOVE YOU despite all what I'm taking you through by being away from you and your Mother. There's only one thing I regret and I would change if I had ONE LAST CHANCE, and that would be to STOP selling dope. I want you to know that me selling dope is the cause and effect of our separation. It's the reason why I'm not in you and your Mother's life. I would never be a snitch. I don't want you to think that if I would of snitched, I would be home. Snitching only amounts to loss of friends, family and relations. Nobody likes or wants to be around a snitch.

And if I did, I would be jeopardizing my life, your life and your Mother' s life. Rats are looked down upon as the lowest scum on earth, to the streets, their family and friends. Son, to be a snitch is to lose integrity, self-pride, dignity and respect. On top of being a snitch and cooperating with the authorities, it does not guarantee your freedom. They did offer me a deal if I was to snitch on other things happening in the city. I don't expect you to want me to take that deal, so that I could come home to you. I expect you to hold your head up and be proud to be a fruit of the real. Let my shortcomings be a lesson to you and make you a better person than me. So, if you're going to be mad, don't be mad because I didn't snitch. Don't be mad because I retaliated on some hating cowards who hurt my family. Be mad because I got in the game. The game is what took me away from you and your Mother. The game is what made me retaliate. The game is what gave me this time.

The game is what I regret, but I accept it because the game is what made me. So I beg you not to get involved in the dope game because it leads to destruction. Destruction of the Black Man and his family. So be mad at the game and stay away from it. I know you and your Mother are struggling and you're right across the street from where it's going down. You're at the age where you're smelling yourself and feel like you can make you and your Mother's situation better, by all means necessary. The best advice I could say to you is stay away from the dope game if you don't want to be in prison, hoping the FEDS will give you ONE LAST CHANCE. They won't, so STOP if you already started.

Love,
    Your one and only father.

Kino balled the letter up, threw it down, and tears started falling from his eyes.

CHAPTER NINETEEN

Poochy and Kino had a meeting with their Manager, Mr. Clydell. He was definitely from the streets. Mr. Clydell went to prison, did his time and got out. He got a job at McDonalds and has been working there ever since, going on ten years. He worked his way up from mopping floors, to the cook, a supervisor, and now he's the manager of this store. He understands the young Black man and could relate to them. Kino and Poochy felt like they could relate to him as well. They felt comfortable speaking the truth to him.

Maybe it was because Mr. Clydell had tattoos and a mouth full of gold. He drove an F-150 with twenty-fours and bumped B.G., Rick Ross, Trick, Jeezy and T.I. He spoke with intelligence that didn't sound nerdy, but cool. He knew his job and was good at managing people, motivating people, and the employees respected him. Mr. Clydell was in his thirties, and cool to work with, as long as you didn't cross him. All he expected is for you to get the job done and don't mess with the money. You do that, then everything is good.

"Damn bro, yall two trippin'. No call, no show, then disappear for a week, show up and expect to have your jobs back," said Mr. Clydell.

Kino thought about his father's letter telling him to keep it real and always speak the truth. "Sir, I know I was wrong. I've been going through a lot and thought I could find a better way to make money quicker to help me and my Mother. I almost got into some serious trouble, but I made it home and read a letter from my Father, who's been in prison since I was born. He told me to leave the streets alone. That' s why I'm here asking you to forgive me and give me one last chance."

Mr. Clydell sits back, looks up at the ceiling, and puts his fingertips from both hands together, then looks at Poochy.

"Sir, a-a-a-s for me, I actually got into some trouble. My Mother had to come and get me from the Juvenile Detention Center. What hurt me the most is the pain I put my Mother through. I just wanted to help her and my Grandpop and selling dope seemed like the best way. Now I see it's not and I hope you will give me another chance, Mr. Clydell.

Their manager stood up and took his shirt off.

He showed them a gunshot wound to his stomach and the scar from surgery because of it. The scar stretched from the bottom of his belly all the way up to his chest. Then he pointed at the scar and said, "This is what the streets did to me. All of my homies who I ran with are either dead, drug addicts, or in prison. And if I wouldn't have stuck to this job, I would be where one of them are today. There's no winning from the streets. Them rappers are rapping a fantasy dream. A nigga's mouth will fry ice cream in them rap songs if you let them tell it. If yall head back to the streets, I promise you it will be too late for whenever or whatever goes down for you to be wishing you had ONE LAST CHANCE. So STOP, now, while you can. I understand where you're coming from. All because you was truthful and kept it real with me, I'm going to give you both one last chance. All I ask for is if you decide to quit for whatever reason, give me a two-week notice and no more no-calls or no-shows. Go clock in and unload the truck that's coming in."

"Thank you Mr. Clydell," both Kino and Poochy tells him.

They're both in the walk-in refrigerator stocking dairy products. Kino asks Poochy, "How did they get you

Poochy?"

"Man, they were coming from everywhere. Every time I got away from one of them, I ran into another one."

"I was about to say you slow as hell. I left they ass. Why you didn't get off the dope?" Kino asked.

"I thought I did, but I forgot about the dope in my other pocket. And they saw me throw the other dope down. They put Derick in the van with me. He told me they choked the shit out of him, He was too high and couldn't react fast enough to swallow the dope, so he spit it out when they started choking him."

"Coupe, Murk and I made it back to the crib. After all that, I ended up reading my old boy's letter," said Kino.

"I heard you tell Mr. Clydell. What'd he say?"

"He said some real Gangster shit. He spoke on keeping it real, don't be a snitch, tell the truth, and stay out the streets if I don't want to be locked up, hoping I had ONE LAST CHANCE. So STOP.

"That's the same thing Mr. Clydell said," replied Poochy.

"I know."

"My Mother made me feel like the worst child a Mother coulda had. I disappointed her and made her cry. She spoke about losing her brothers to the game and almost my Father and it will kill her if she loses me," Poochy says.

"Hand me them cases of cheese," Kino tells him.

"I got ya. Man, whoever stocked this did not F.I.F.O. it

"When I finish stacking these boxes of cheese I'll come help ya. We got to do it right and leave a good impression on Mr. Clydell," Kino tells Poochy.

"Kino, I can't go back to selling dope because I don't want to hurt my Mother again."

"I believe my Father, Poochy. He told me he's still fighting his case and I can't be locked up when he comes home. I'm not going back either."

CHAPTER TWENTY

Kino and Poochy are on their lunch break at work.

"You talked to Tanisha?" Poochy asks Kino.

"Yeah, and I hung up on her ass." Kino is too embarrassed to tell Poochy she hung up on him. Then he thought about his Dad's words and recants his statement.

"Nah, she hung up on me bro."

"After all you did for her and she hung up on you?" Poochy says, then starts laughing. "Damn bro, that's messed up," Poochy said in a joking voice.

Kino still has feelings for her and doesn't want Poochy to see her as someone bad, so he takes up for her and says, "I called her a tricking-ass hoe who plays games and that's why she hung up on me."

"I told Shawana she was a gold-digging hoe and she got mad at me and said she didn't want to talk about Tanisha no more.

But maybe you should call Tanisha and apologize to her bro," Poochy said.

"I got jumped because of Tanisha and you want me to call and apologize to her?"

Poochy punches Kino on the shoulder and says, "Stop playing hard nigga, you know you want to call her. Now what if she's telling the truth and she's not no hoe. Then you owe her a big apology. If yall make up, we can double date. You know girls let loose when they more comfortable. And they more comfortable when they're with their friend."

"Alright, I'll call her for you," Kino says as he laughs while Poochy laughs along with him. Both of them know Kino is flossin'.

****

The telephone is ringing; Tanisha answers the phone.

"What's up Shawana?"

"Girl, you."

"What you need now Shawana?" Tanisha says sarcastically.

"You talked to Kino?" Shawana asks.

"Not since I hung up on him."

"You need to call that nigga back."

"For what? He called me a tricking-ass hoe."

"Tanisha, what nigga you know stands up to Dae'Quan on top of doing it for you? That nigga loves you. Let him know it was all a misunderstanding and invite him on a date to make up for that night at the club."

Tanisha has feelings for Kino just as much as he has for her. But she's not as stubborn as Kino.

"Where would I take him?" Tanisha asks.

"On a picnic. Me and Poochy are going and you and Kino can tag along."

"Where yall going on a picnic to?"

"Rock Springs. We can barbecue on the grill and walk the trail and get to know each other."

"This him calling on the other line now," Tanisha says.

"I'll holla. Let me know because I need to use your food stamps to buy the food."

"Girl, I knew you were up to something. Bye!"

Tanisha clicks over.

"Hello."

"What's up Tanisha?"

"What you want Kino, because I'm not going to sit up here and listen to you call me no hoe!"

"That's why I called."

"What!"

"No, don't hang up! To apologize."

"Oh," she says, as she takes a deep breath.

- A pause of silence –

"I'm sorry, I'm sorry Tanisha for calling you a hoe."

"Kino I understand why you might think that, but you shoulda had more patience and gave me a chance to explain myself before you came to that conclusion."

"Well what happened?"

"I was young and dumb three years ago when I was fifteen. He filled my head with lies and took advantage of me.

When I gave up my goodies, he became a possessive controlling abusive boyfriend who I ended up getting pregnant by. My Mother was going to press charges on him for rape because he was over eighteen, but I begged her not to. I wanted my little girl to have her daddy instead of being locked up. After a while I couldn't' be in a relationship no more with him. When I stopped giving up the goodies, he stopped taking care of his daughter, no money, no time, no nothing with her."

"So why was he tripping at the club?" Kino asks.

"Shawana wanted to go to the club on baller status. Free ride, free drinks, free V.I. P., so she persuaded me to let him take us. You give a nigga an inch and he'll take a mile.   He figured he owns me since he paid for everything. I knew I shouldn't of went with him because I don't like him and we're not together. So I apologize to you Kino. I want to be straight up with you. I should not of went with him just to ball in the club. That is not me and I'm sorry."

Kino almost fainted. He never met a female so real. She admitted her shortcomings, apologizing for them, learning from them, and striving to become better. This is the exact female he's been searching for, one who can be truthful to herself and then to him.

"You don't have to be sorry. You are far from being a hoe. You are a true, strong, beautiful Black Queen. One who is intelligent, sexy, and cute. Brains with a body and a heart of real. I feel special talking to you now."

Then a pause of silence on the phone. Simultaneously they both say, "You want to…"

"Ladies first," Kino says.

"What was you about to say?" asks Tanisha.

"I said ladies first," Kino said, in a demanding voice.

"Aight Mr. Man. You want to go on a picnic with Shawana and Poochy?"

"I'll go anywhere with you," Kino says.

"OK, let me find out what time and day and I'll call you back."

"I'll be waiting."

"Bye."

"I'll holla." (click)

Shawana is calling Poochy and he answers the phone.

"Hello."

"What's up baby?"

"What's up Shawana?"

"We still on for Saturday?" Shawana asks.

"Yeah," Poochy answered.

"Do you mind if Tanisha and Kino come along?"

"I was going to ask you the same thing. It's all good." Poochy says.

"What time yall picking us up?" Shawana asks. She does not know that Poochy nor Kino owns a car. Poochy is too embarrassed to let her know that he does not have a car, so he tells her, "Twelve o'clock."

"That's perfect, I'll make sure Tanisha is here with me."

"I'll see ya," Poochy says.

"Bye bae." (click)

Poochy is thinking "What am I going to do?" He calls Kino and he answers.

"What's up Pooch?"

"Kino, I got some good news and some bad news. Which

one do you want to hear first?"

"Give me the good news."

"Tanisha is going to come with Shawana and she wants you to come."

"I already know that, you late we been talked. So what's the bad news?"

"We got to pick them up."

"In what?" Kino asks in a crazy sounding voice. "That's why I called you."

"I thought Murk do dumb things, nah, let me take that back, Murk do crazy things, you do dumb things," Kino replied.

"Oh! Oh! Oh! Charley!" Poochy spits out.

"Big money Charley?" Kino asks.

"Yeah, let's rent his car for the day."

"We don't got no dope and we both staying away from over there," Kino reminded Poochy.

"Murk and Coupe still be over there grinding."

Murk walks in the house and asks Kino, "Is that Poochy? Tell him I said what's up and yall missing that moolah."

"Murk said what's up Poochy."

"Let me holla at him," Poochy tells Kino.

Kino calls Murk and hands him the phone. "Here, Poochy wants to holla at ya." Murk gets the phone from Kino.

"What's up bra-bra?" Murk says.

"You think you can get Charley's car Saturday?" asks Poochy. "Yeah, we had it yesterday."

"Me and Kino going on a date."

"I know it ain't them hoes yall was with at the club who we got kicked out for."

"Yeah, it's them," Poochy told Murk.

"Good, fuck the shit out of them hoes. Fuck them niggas!" Murk said laughing.

"They ain't no hoes!" Kino says, then snatched the phone from Murk.

"Damn, I know you ain't getting mad. Nigga, you in love?" Murk says as he walks out the room laughing. Kino gets back on the phone.

"When Murk gets the car I'll come and get ya. What time you told them we picking them up?"

"Twelve o'clock."

"Murk will get the car in the morning and I'll be to your house at eleven."

"Aight."

"I'll holla."

****

Beer bottles, left over fast food still in the bags, along with everyday trash piled up on the floors; cigarette burns in the seats and greasy door handles. The steering wheel and all the leather in the car is a shade darker than the original color from the dirt of the hands of a mechanic.

Charley was a truck mechanic and made big money working on truck engines. He would also get the trucker's money who were passing through, then go to the hood and buy dope for them. If he wasn't working, he was smoking. If he wasn't spending his money, he's buying for other truckers.

This is why they called him Big Money Charley. His car had a stench of mechanic funk, smoked crack, and cigarettes, all combined in one. You had to be either drunk, high on weed, or a smoker yourself to endure the smell. Other than that, it will make you throw up. The outside looked decent, so if you never got inside, you would not know the extent of the filth that laid within the car.

Saturday morning at 9:00 a.m. Murk pulls in Peppertree Apartments in a Mercury Grand Marquis looking like a police car. He calls Kino on the phone to come out and get the car so he could go back across the street to the Palms Apartments. Kino looks at Murk.

"You look like you been up all night, and what' s that White stuff on your nose?"

Murk started hawking from the drain of cocaine then said, "I was eating a powdered jelly donut." He took his hand, wiped his nose and hawked again. He threw Kino the keys and said, "I'll holla," then left for the Palms Apartments.

Kino caught the keys as he looked at Murk walking away then yelled, "How much money I owe you?"

"Nothing bra, have fun."

Kino kept staring at him as he was walking away, knowing Murk is up to no good and has started snorting cocaine. Kino starts to worry about Murk. He opens the car door and the stench damn near knocked him out. He looks on the floor and sees chicken bones, beer cans and trash. Even some dirty flip flop shoes on the back seat.

"We can't pick them girls up in this," he says to himself. He rides down to Winn Dixie to cash his check, then goes to Magic Mall and get the car detailed. He goes back home to get dressed. He calls Poochy and tells him he's going to pick the girls up first and him last since he lives in Apopka, closer to Rock Springs. Kino left his house to pick up the ladies.

Telephone ringing.

"Hello."

"What's up Tanisha? I'm a couple of minutes away. I'm in a gray Grand Marquis with tinted windows."

"We'll be outside," Tanisha told him.

Kino pulls into Beirut and parks. Before you know it, ten niggas done rushed the car. When they get close up and see that it's not Charley, they back away.

"This ain't no money," Tanisha yells at them.

"Alright now, don't let Dae'Quan catch your ass."

"Dae'Quan don't own this." She slaps her ass and it jiggles as she walks in a sunflower dress. All the hustlers say "Damn that ass fat."

"Shut up Do-boy," Shawana says getting in the car.

"Chickenhead!" he yells as Kino drives away. Tanisha and Shawana look at each other.

"Damn, what's that smell?" Shawana says.

"It smells like somebody who's funky, but instead of them taking a bath, they just put on deodorant and cologne to try to hide the smell," says Tanisha.

"It smells like a baser's car. This your car Kino?" Shawana asks.

"Nah, this ain't my car."

Tanisha knew he wasn't a dope dealer. He didn't have any gold in his mouth, he worked at McDonalds, his clothes weren't expensive and he didn't have jewelry. He looked like a regular person, which is what she wanted. Shawana just wanted someone who didn't try to use her for her goodies. Tanisha tried to ease Kino's worries, because she sensed him being embarrassed.

"It's OK Kino, I'm just glad you came and got me so we can be together." Kino looked at her and smiled as his anxiety decreased. They picked up Poochy in Lake Jewel, then headed for Rock Springs.

"Pull over at this gas station and let's get some inner tubes," said Shawana.

"I'm not getting in no water and I don't have no clothes anyway," said Tanisha.

"Party pooper, your ass getting in," said Shawana.

"I don't got no extra clothes either," Kino says.

"Don't even trip bro, I got an extra pair of swimming trunks," Poochy told Kino.

"Tanisha, remember when we were in your room and your Mother called you outside to help her with your daughter?" Shawana asked.

"Yeah."

"I went through your drawers and got your bathing suit and I brought an extra big T-shirt so you don't have no excuse either." Poochy and Shawana high-five each other and start laughing.

"Yall think yall slick," Kino says looking at Poochy. They all start laughing.

They rent two inner tubes, buy a few items, tie the tubes down to the roof of the car then head for the park. After carrying everything from the car to the table, Kino and Poochy sit down.

"What yall cooking? Yall supposed to be catering to us, but we carrying these big ass inner tubes, basket, coolers, and charcoal..." Poochy says.

"What yall barbecuing?" asks Kino.

"Yall just sit back and enjoy. We got this," Shawana says.

"What I really need is a massage for all that ass I was whooping for you in the club," Kino says.

"You can get that too boo, I got ya," Tanisha replied.

"That's what I'm talking about," Kino said in a confident voice.

Poochy looks at Shawana and she says, "Don't look at me, you weren't fighting for me." Poochy throws a balled up napkin at her and she screams, "Stop!" They all start laughing.

"My boy wasn't going to let me get jumped, so he fought for me. I know he woulda did the same for you so give him some play," Kino told Shawana.

Tanisha has to get back at Shawana for bringing Tanisha's bathing suit, so she adds on to Kino's speech. "Shawana, I know you're not going to leave me hanging. If I'm going to get in the water, you got to give Poochy a massage."

"Alright, I got ya," Shawana says in a pouting voice.

Poochy and Kino look at each other and nod their heads with a smile.

Tanisha and Shawana do everything. They light the charcoal and get the fire started, then pull out six potatoes wrapped in aluminum foil, then put them directly under the grill with the charcoal.

"Ain't that going to burn the potatoes," Kino asks.

"No fool, that's why they're wrapped in that foil," says Poochy.

The women pull out corn on the cob, chicken already seasoned, four steaks, then place them on the grill. They also have some baked beans, cooked with ground turkey meat, sugar and chunks of turkey sausage cut up in it. It was pre-cooked so all it had to be was warmed up. Dinner rolls from Winn Dixie and a big bowl of homemade salad, made with lettuce, cucumbers, diced tomatoes, broccoli florets, chopped green onions, cut up red and green bell peppers, topped with chopped toasted cashews, sunflower seed, raisins and garlic croutons.

"Where's the ranch dressing Shawana?" Tanisha asked.

"It should be next to the Italian dressing. "

"Kino, can you put this cooler on the table?" Tanisha asked. "Yeah, what yall got to drink?"

"Tea, Coke, bottled water and punch my Aunty made," Tanisha says.

"Let me see what this punch like."

Poochy sees some older people he knows from Apopka and they set up next to them.

After the ladies prep all the food and cook it, they went to the restroom to get into their bathing suits. Rock Springs has a mild atmosphere with families, couples, older people and children. That's why Tanisha and Shawana wore a long T-shirt over their two-piece bathing suits. Black women have a lot of junk in their trunk. Walking around in that type of environment would draw the wrong type of attention.

Kino looks at Tanisha every chance he gets when she's not looking. Every time he sees that ass wiggle as it grips the T-shirt and bounce with every step she takes, he just shakes his head and says to himself, "Damn, I can't wait to tear that pussy up."

Poochy runs up and smacks Shawana's ass. She slaps him back and says, "Stop playing boy," smiling at the same time. Shawana asks them, "Yall ready?"

"For what?" Kino asks.

"To ride the inner tubes down the stream."

Poochy jumps up and says, "Let's go." Kino and Tanisha look at each other and take a deep breath.

"Come on Tanisha, we here now," Shawana says.

Rock Springs has a starting point in a cave. The water flows down in a river pattern into a pond area where everybody swims. It continues all throughout Florida, connecting with other springs in other cities.

They grab their tubes and roll them up a bridge-like sidewalk made from wood. It is a trail through the woods alongside the spring that traverses all the way to the beginning of the spring where the cave is. They all go down the steps that lead to the water. Poochy is from Apopka where Rock Springs is so he's been there plenty of times. He jumps in to get the coldness process over with. If you try to walk in slow, it will feel like you're walking into an ice pool. Jumping in is the best method to get used to the cold water quickly. Poochy holds the tube steady so Shawana can get on top of it. She calls herself easing in slow.

"It's cold," Shawana yells.

Poochy takes his arm and slaps the water, making a big splash that sends water directly down Shawana's neck and back. She screams, turns around and splashes him back. Now it's a splash fight in the water and Tanisha hauls ass down the trail while Shawana and Poochy are laughing at each other. They finally stop splashing each other, then she gets on the tube with her butt in the middle and her arms and legs hanging over the inner tube. Poochy is in waist deep holding on to the tube, steering her wherever he wants to take her. If he lets her go she will float downstream away from him, so he holds on to her waiting for Kino and Tanisha to join them so they can all go down the stream together.

"Come on Tanisha!" yells Shawana, looking at her from far away.

"Come on girl!" yells Kino. He grabs her hand and walks her down the steps into the water. Kino takes the first step in, saying "Damn it's cold as ice!"

Tanisha thinks she's slick and pushes Kino to make him fall in the ice cold water. Kino is keen and has quick reflexes. So quick, that when she pushes him, he grabs her on his way falling, bringing her with him. She screams and they both fall in - all the way in. Poochy and Shawana are cracking up. When they ascend from the water, she slapped him. Kino grabbed her, she struggled to get away, but she couldn't. Something came over Kino and he kissed her. She kissed him back. Tanisha shifted three gears in three seconds. She went from mad as hell to laughing at herself and Kino, to passionate intimacy as they locked lips, tongue kissing, holding each other.

"Aye! Aye! Get a hotel for that," says Poochy.
"I'm telling you," Shawana yells.
"Come get this tube Kino," Poochy held their tube so it would not float downstream.

Kino grabs it and walks it over to Tanisha and he holds it while she gets in it. Kino and Poochy push them downstream through the crystal clear water. The spring is about ten feet wide in the middle of the woods, a habitat for bears, deer, snakes, raccoons, Florida Panthers, and a host of other animals.

The scenery is beautiful.
"Is that a fish?" says Tanisha.
"Look, a turtle!" says Shawana.
"Ah, he's so cute," says Tanisha.
"There's snakes in here too," Poochy tells them, then he says, "Yall get out," as he pushes Shawana to the edge of the spring.

A path that's about two feet wide breaks off from the main part of the spring. As Poochy leads the way treading through knee-high deep water, other people pass by from where they're going. Kino and the girls follow Poochy to the end and it looks like a pond where boiling water is coming up from underground.

"This is a spring, see the water coming from under the ground?"

Poochy tells them. A loud scream comes from Shawana as she jumps on Poochy's back. She screams so loud she scared Kino. Tanisha did exactly what we do in the club. One person starts running, you start running. You don't even know why you're running. You're just running because the next person is running. So Tanisha jumps on Kino's back too.

"Why you screaming?" Poochy asks.
"A snake," Shawana says.
"Where?"
"Over there," she points, still on Poochy' s back.
"He gone now. I don't see him," Poochy says.

The girls get back in their tubes and the boys push them down the stream. This time Poochy goes under and ascends in the center of the tube facing Shawana, steering her now whichever way he walks. They hold each other at the same time and he kisses her. They arrive at a part where people snorkel for shark teeth. They all go up under a bridge and enter the swimming area. Here the spring goes from ten feet wide to a medium size pond with a depth of about ten feet. At this spot Poochy tells Shawana, "Tanisha went all the way, now it's your turn." Then Poochy overturns the inner tube, dunking her under the water. Tanisha looks at Kino and points her finger at him waving it from right to left, shaking her head saying in a sassy voice, "Don't you even think about it." He tugs on the tube like he's going to dunk her, playing with her, but he doesn't flip her over. Kino is swimming, his feet no longer touch bottom. Tanisha stays on the tube.

Poochy and Kino swim across, while Kino pushes Tanisha until they all get to the part of the spring where they can wade through the water. They get out of the water there and are only a few feet away from their table. The girls walk back while Kino and Poochy roll the inner tubes up to the tables.

"Thanks Mr. Cobb," Poochy tells the family he knows for watching their food and things while they went to the water.

They all dry off. Kino and Poochy sit at the table while the women fix their plates. Kino feels like a king. This is the first and only woman who had ever cooked for him and fixed his plate, besides his Mother. Tanisha brought him his food and asked him, "What do you want to drink?" Kino tells her some more of that homemade punch her Aunty made. He watches Tanisha walk as the wet T-shirt grips her body, revealing her shape. Kino and Poochy haven't had sex with the girls yet and they are already sprung. Food is definitely a way to a man's heart, and these young women definitely know how to cook.

They all ate until their stomachs were full. Kino says, "What's up with the massage?" Tanisha gets up and picks up all the plates and trash, washes her hands, then tells Shawana to get the blanket out. She spreads the blanket and goes into her purse and pulls some lotion out, then tells Kino to lay down. Kino looks at Poochy and smiles with a smirk on his face, then he started rapping Ludacris's song to rub it in on Poochy. "*My chick bad, my chick good, my chick does things that your chick wish she could.*"

Kino lays down on his stomach and Tanisha sits on top of him, squeezing lotion on her hand and his back, then went to work. When Tanisha started massaging Kino's back, Poochy said, "Hell no, move over Kino," and got on the other half of the blanket, laid down on his stomach, then lifted his head up and looked back at Shawana. Kino and Tanisha bust out laughing. Shawana rolled her eyes back, looked at Poochy, shook her head and smiled, because he was funny, then said, "I'm coming bae, hold your horses."

Shawana gets on top of Poochy and asks Tanisha for the lotion, then went to work.

CHAPTER TWENTY-ONE

D-Bo is sitting on his bed reading the Bible when his cell door opens up. A bald-headed big bearded man walks in and says, "What's up?" He extends his hand out for a fist dap. "My name is 'Abdush-Shukar.''

"My name is Derick Betterman, they call me D-Bo." D-Bo looks at his new celly's attire. The bottom of his pants legs were raised above his ankles.

"You bringing back the 70's, high-water, huh?" D-Bo says as they both laugh.

"Nah bra, Prophet Muhammad, salallaahu alayhi wa sallam, said, "Whatever of the izzar, meaning the clothes covering the body, comes lower than the ankles is in the fire." He, salallahu alayhi wa sallam, also said, "Beware of letting the garment come below the ankles, for that is conceit and Allah does not like conceit."

D-Bo then asks him, "How is wearing your pants below the ankle being conceited?"

"During the contemporary time of Prophet Muhammad, salallahu alayhi wa sallam, the disbelieving idol worshippers would wear their garments below their ankles out of pride and arrogance. Their pride prevented them from believing in the ONENESS of Allah and accepting Prophet Muhammad, salallahu alayhi wa sallam, as the last and final messenger sent to all mankind. This will result in them being sentenced to the Hellfire on the Day of Judgment. The Prophet, salallahu alayhi wa sallam, commanded his companions to be different from the disbelievers. We as Muslims believe in him, follow him, obey him, and adhere to his guidance until the Last Day. Not like some people assume that Muhammad's, salallahu alayhi wa sallam, ways are only for his contemporary time.

"What is that you be saying every time you mention Muhammad's name?" asks D- Bo.

"You mean salallahu alayhi wa sallam?"

"Yeah."

"It means 'peace and prayers be upon him.' Allah The Most High commands us in the Qur'an in surah 33:56 to send prayers and peace upon Muhammad every time his name is mentioned. When we say 'salallahu alayhi' it means 'prayers upon him,' meaning invoking Allah to commend him and mention his high status to the angels. When we say 'wa sallam,' it means 'and peace which is security for him.'"

"So you have to say that every time Prophet Muhammad's name is mentioned?" D-Bo asks.

"Yes, and you get blessings for saying it. So now you know whenever you hear a Muslim telling another Muslim, "Your pants are in the fire," you know what he means."

D-Bo thought to himself how serious this Muslim believed, he followed and obeyed Muhammad all the way to their dress code.

"I pray to Jesus and God. Who is Allah? I heard he was some moon God," D-Bo asks the Muslim.

"We Muslims worship the God of Adam, the God of Abraham, Noah, Moses, Jesus and all the Prophets and Messengers, peace be upon all of them, that was sent to mankind. 'Allah' means 'The God' in Arabic, meaning the ONE and only Creator of the universe and everything that exists. There are Arabs who are Jews and Christians who refer to the Creator as Allah, not God, because they speak Arabic. The King James version of the Bible, translated into Arabic, calls the Creator Allah, not God. We as Muslims worship the same deity who the Christians and the Jews worship. The difference is that we don't associate any partners with Allah. We don't worship Jesus, alayhi wa sallam. That expression, alayhi wa sallam' means 'peace be upon him.'

D- Bo admired his loyalty to following Muhammad, but when he thought Muslims didn't worship and believe in Jesus like his Mother and Grandma taught him, he said to himself, "All what they do for God will be in vain because they're going to hell for not believing in Jesus."

"I got some extra soap if you need some," D-Bo tells him.

"Thanks, but baytalmal will take care of me."

"What's baytalmal?" D-Bo asks him.

"A collection of items for the indigent Muslims and the new brothers who just got on the compound."

Another Muslim comes to the room and gives 'Abdush-Shukar the full greeting – "As-salaamu alaykum wa rahma tu Allah wa baraka tuhu." 'Abdush-Shukar returns the greeting, puts up his things, then leaves with the other Muslim to go to get some items from baytalmal.

CHAPTER TWENTY-TWO

Coupe and Murk are on the block in the second breezeway hustling.

"What's up with Poochy and Kino? I see why Poochy quit hustling, he still got to go to JV court, but why Kino stop serving?" asks Coupe.

"He told me something about a letter from his Father. wish my father would write me," Murk told Coupe.

"All my dad cares about is trying to be like T.D. Jakes. He don't care about me."

Coupe's phone rings.

"Oh shoot! This Quanita," Coupe says.

"The doctor's daughter?" asks Murk.

"Yeah."

"Answer it, you scared?" Murk asks Coupe.

"Hello."

"Why you haven't been answering your phone? I've been worried about you," she said to Coupe.

"I've been busy, but I'm good now. Girl, you sure that wasn't a bad pill you gave me?"

"I told you to take half, but nah, you wanted to take the whole pill," she starts laughing. Coupe starts getting mad and she senses it in his voice.

"Let me make it up to you boo," she says.

"How you gonna do that?"

"My girl's throwing a private party. Bring your homeboys, and after the party I'm all yours."

"As long as you don't have none of that bull crap," he says.

She giggles then says, "I won't."

"Aight, I gotta burn this block up, you got me missing money already. "

"Bye boo," she said.

"I'll holla." (click)

Murk comes running back from a serve and he tells Coupe, "Mont just knocked out a jug in the third breezeway."

"Why?" asks Coupe.

"Something about the jug had some counterfeit money. That nigga box. I'll have to shoot his ass."

"They say he be knocking niggas out at the club every time Mercy Drive get into it with somebody."

Coupe takes out an eight ball, slices it up with his finger-nail into all twenties.

"I cut one eighty out of this ball." Coupe says.

"They say Crosstown has so much dope you got to cut big pieces. They only cutting one forty to one sixty of a ball. But in Pinehills they cutting two to two-fifty of a ball," one of the hustlers on the block told Coupe and Murk.

Coupe is now gumlining. He put the whole eight ball cut up in his mouth. A car pulls up, Murk and Coupe run at the car racing each other for the sale. The car does not stop in the middle of the street, instead the car parks, then backs out in reverse, then they pull out like they're leaving and ask for Booby.

"Booby ain't here," Coupe tells them.

"You got a hundred?" the baser asks.

Coupe walks out to the middle of the parking lot to the car and spits the dope from his mouth into his hands, then shows him five twenties.

"Let me get another twenty?" the baser asks Coupe.

"You want six twenties for a hundred?"

"That's what Booby gives me."

"Aight."

Coupe gives the jug another twenty. The baser has all the dope in his hand and tells Coupe to hold up while he reaches into his pocket to pull the money out. As soon as Coupe looks up at this chick that was at Fee-Fee's house walking to Lee's store, the jug hit it on Coupe burning rubber - "eerrrr" skid sounds as the car takes off. Coupe chases the car, slapping the window with his hand, almost getting run over, as they hit the curve and haul ass out of the Palms. Coupe looks at them ride away.

Murk says, "Damn, I shoulda brought my gun!" Coupe comes back breathing hard. The other niggas on the block are asking what happened. Derick and Pete came running, asking Coupe what's up. Booby came from around the building.

"Booby, the jug was asking for you," Coupe tells him.

"Was they in a blue Honda?"

"Yep."

"They been spinning all night, they probably ran out of money," Booby told them.

Murk asks Coupe if he was straight, then him, Pete and Derick went to find a jug to send to the ABC liquor store to get them some Gray Goose because Old Man Paul who sells the bootleg liquor wasn't home. He's usually available late night after the club, and when everything else is closed. Coupe sold the rest of his dope then went to his car to leave and go home.

He parked in the Palms Apartments instead of Peppertree. When he left out of the apartments, the police were watching everything pulling out of the projects. They got behind him and pulled him over.

"License and registration," the officer told him.

"May I ask whatcha pull me over for?"

"Speeding," the officer told him.

"How was I speeding when I just pulled out the

125

apartments?"

"Do you have any drugs or   guns in the vehicle?"

"No."

"Can I search your vehicle?"

"No!"

"OK, I need you to wait for the dogs. Step out please. If you're clean, you will be on your way."

Coupe stands at the back of his car while the officer goes to his police car and calls for the dogs. The dispatcher comes back and says, "Red Toyota Corolla involved in a shooting in Pinehills. Back windshield was shot out of the car. Only four numbers and letters of the license plate were remembered by the witness. Car registered to Curtis Placky who you have in custody fits the description, along with the four digits given for the plate numbers."

He walks back to Coupe and says, "Were you in Pinehills last week?"

"I live in Pinehills, you know this."

"Let me be more specific. Was your car involved in a shooting in Pinehills?"

"I ain't shot no one."

"I didn't say that. Did your back window get shot out?"

"NO!" Coupe said in a frustrated voice.

Four other police cars pull up. They bring a dog out. They walk the dog around the car. As soon as the dog gets to the door, he barks and scratches as if there are drugs in the car.

We all know that here in the Dirty South the police are dirty and make the dogs bark. I don't smoke, nor do I allow smoking in my car. Yet so many times I've been clean and told the police they can't search the car, so they bring out the dogs, and of course he barks, sits, scratches or whatever they make him do to indicate that there's drugs in the car. But when they search the car, they don't find any drugs. Then the cop tells me, "Oh someone was smoking weed in my car, that's why the dog barked." They were just lying their asses off.

When the dog indicated that there were drugs in the car, the officer walked up to Coupe and said, "I'm going to place you in handcuffs for your safety during the search. If everything is clean we will let you go."

They placed Coupe in the back seat as he watched them tear his car up. Coupe sold all the dope he had left, so he knows there are no drugs in the car nor does he own a gun.

The officer comes back to his police car and gets on the radio.

"Can we have a tow truck here on Mercy Drive by the Palms Apartments?" He turns to Coupe and says, "You're under arrest for cruelty to animals and attempted murder."

"What the hell?" Coupe said in shock.

Kino got out of school. Him, Murk and half the Palms Apartments tenants are out looking at Coupe. Kino says to Murk, "He must of had some dope in the car."

"Nah, Booby's jug spinned off with his dope and I think he sold the rest."

Somebody who was watching the whole scene and walked by them said, "They pulled something small out the back seat, then I heard the officers talking about some broken glass, a credit card, and the mention of a bullet."

Coupe was taken to the 33rd and placed in a holding cell, as cold as the North Pole. He was charged as an adult because of the severity of his case, which is why they didn't take him to J.V. Coupe looks and notices the same transit who sleeps in a cardboard box house in the woods behind Winn Dixie supermarket. He does not know these jugs, but he can tell they're smokers. He sees hustlers his age and older. All of them have a mouth full of gold, some bald heads, some dreads, and some with mohawks.

Balled up in a corner, he sees an old White man crying, yelling. "I didn't mean to hurt her! I love her!"

A medium built, low cut, shadow bearded, clean dressed Black man comes in. As soon as the police walk away from the door, he goes in his pants, digging by his nuts and pulls out a bag full of powder, pours it into the toilet, then flushes it. An officer comes to the window and yells - "Curtis Placky." The door slides open and Coupe steps out.

"Open cell block ten," the C.O. yells to the Control Center. Another cell opens. Coupe steps in and the officer follows behind him.

"Strip search. Everything off," the C.O. tells him. Coupe takes everything off and is shivering from the cold temperature and shock of his first arrest.

"Open your mouth, tongue out, turn around, squat, cough, bottom of your feet. Put your clothes back on." Coupe comes out the cell. "Over here," another C.O. calls to him. "Let me see your hand." He takes something that looks like a paint roller that's Black. He rolls ink on Coupe's hand. "Right thumb," the C.O. tells him. Coupe gets fingerprinted, his height measured, his picture taken, checked over by a nurse, and then interviewed.

"Can I get a phone call?"

"As soon as we are through," the officer told Coupe. They give him his arresting papers then send him back to another cell that has a phone.

"Who's last?" Coupe asks.

"I am," a Mexican with tattoos all over his body, his head, neck and face says.

"I'm after you," Coupe tells him.

Coupe sits on the cold, hard, concrete bench, looks around and sees people sleeping on the floor, using toilet tissue as a pillow. The jugs smell like death's coming out of them. He opens up his arresting papers, curious about his charge. He knows about Murk killing the dogs. He's wondering how in the world he got an attempted murder charge. The paper read:

"Pulled arrestee Curtis Placky over for speeding. I smelled marijuana emanating from the car. Upon taking arrestee's license and registration, I ran the license plate and the vehicle came back as a suspect in a shooting in Pinehills. A narcotic K-9 was called because arrestee refused to allow a search of the vehicle. The dog alerted as to narcotics in the vehicle. Upon searching the vehicle, evidence connecting arrestee to the shooting was found. Glass particles from a broken back windshield. Exhibit 1. In a deep crevice in the back seat I found a bullet which is being sent to the lab to see if it matches the gun of ex-police officer Bill Mayers, owner of dogs killed. Exhibit 2. A credit card was also found and a nationwide check will be done to see if the card is stolen. Exhibit 3." Coupe kept reading, the report continued:

"Bill Mayers claims that after suspects shot and killed his dogs, they shot at him which is why he shot back at the suspects, shooting out the rear window of the escape vehicle."

Coupe blurted out loud, "Hell no! Ain't nobody shoot at his ass.

I wasn't speeding, and that cop knows damn well he didn't smell no weed!"

The truth is always different... Bill Mayers had to make up that lie to cover his ass. He needed a reason why he shot at them when they left the scene and were no longer a threat to him.

As for the police, they need probable cause for pulling Coupe over, calling the dogs, and searching the car. The officer lied and said Coupe was speeding, giving him reason for pulling him over. He claimed that he smelled weed which gave him the probable cause for calling the dogs. And the officer who brought the dog made the dog bark, giving the officer probable cause to search the vehicle. Even though they didn't find any drugs or a weapon, Coupe is now booked on two counts: cruelty to animals and attempted murder. After calling his Mother, he called Kino and told him the charges.

CHAPTER TWENTY-THREE

Mrs. Placky and Pastor Placky are in a heated argument about their son Curtis.

"When are we going to bond Curtis out?" Mrs. Placky asks her husband.

"How much is his bond?" he asks.

"A hundred thousand for all the charges. Ten thousand to get him out, and we have to sign the house over until he goes to court."

"Hell no, that boy shoulda thought about the consequences before he did what he did."

"Jamal! He said he didn't do it!" Mrs. Placky screamed at him.

"What's he doing on Mercy Drive anyway? If he didn't do it, then why did they arrest him? His ass need to learn a lesson. God don't like ugly."

"Why are you claiming our son is guilty like the White man does? You didn't even try to listen to him when he called. You just blamed him. We are his parents, and are supposed to be there for him, rather he's wrong or right. I'm not telling you to support his wrong doings, but if he is at fault, we shouldn't turn our backs on him either. Besides that, we don't even know if he's innocent or not.

"Ten thousand dollars!" Pastor Placky reiterated. "I'm trying to extend and remodel the church so I can attract more people. I don't have any extra money to be running behind

Curtis. Money spent on God is better than spending it on an evil son."

"Jamal! You son of a bitch! How dare you call our son evil! You sure know how to use them Bible verses to your benefit!" She slammed the door and left the house crying. Mrs. Placky already knew the whole problem is money. It's not about whether their son is right or wrong, or just being there for him. All Pastor Placky cares about is money and fame.

****

Kino, Murk and Poochy are outside of Peppertree Apartments leaning on the wall. A donk rides by on twenty sixes, jamming Plies song, "*Pussy ass crackers give a nigga a hundred years. Have your momma leaving out the courtroom in tears...*" Murk takes a swig from a Heineken bottle then says, "I'm gonna buy me one of them old school Chevy's and paint it Black. Everything Black."

Poochy asks Kino, "What they gonna do with Coupe?"

"He called me and said they charged him with cruelty to animals and attempt to murder."

"Attempt to murder! How in the world did he get them charges?"

"The owner of the dogs Murk killed said we shot at him and tried to kill him. So they charged Coupe for killing the dogs and shooting at the owner."

"Ain't nobody shoot at his ass," Poochy said.

"Nah, but we can!" says Murk.

"When his parents gonna bond him out?" asks Poochy.

"Coupe told me his Father is tripping and don't care nothing about him."

"How much is his bond?" asks Murk.

"Ten thousand to get him out, and twenty-five thousand for a lawyer."

Murk comes off the wall he was leaning on and looks Poochy and Kino in the eyes, then says, "What we gonna do?" He's feeling guilty because he was the one who shot the dogs, even though he was only defending Kino.

"What we supposed to do?" asks Kino.

"Get this money and get him out," says Poochy.

"I'll just go and rob T. He owe you anyway," says Murk.

"No, ain't nobody gonna rob nobody," says Kino.

"Then we got to get it on the block Kino," says Poochy.

"Poochy, you already have a charge pending on you and what about your Mother? You already forgot how you made her feel? Murk, if I go to jail or get killed out there in the streets, who's going to take care of Mom and look after your crazy ass?"

"Ain't nothing gonna happen to you while I'm breathing. Let's just make this money, then get out. If not, I'm going to get it the best way I know how," Murk tells Kino. Kino walks off mad and confused.

"Where you going?" asks Poochy.

"To the store. I'll be right back," Kino told them.

All four of them grew up together since Ivy Lane Elementary School. Although their parents moved away from each other, the boys always managed to keep in contact with each other. Now as teenagers, they all go to Evans High School, except for Murk. Poochy uses Coupe's home address in Pinehills so he could attend Evans High School with Kino and Coupe. Coupe would drive all the way to Apopka every morning to pick Poochy up for school. These four were inseparable. Kino wants to bring Coupe home just as bad as they do. The difference is that Kino is more conscious of the consequences than they are. His father's letter had a big influence on him, especially when he said, "You don't want to be in prison wishing you had ONE LAST CHANCE," keeps ringing in his head.

On his way walking to the store, he thought about how Murk would try to do something stupid to get Coupe out of jail. He also thought that if he didn't help Coupe, he would end up going to prison for a long time for something he didn't do, messing with those public Pretenders just like his

Father. Kino also felt somewhat guilty because it was him who the dogs were attacking, which is why Murk shot the dogs in the first place. Then he thought about how Poochy would try and do it all by himself, making Kino feel less than a friend if he sat back and did nothing while everybody else tried.

Believe it or not, this dilemma that Kino is going through happens every day in every city all over the country. These young men have no guidance. So now they guide themselves the best and the only way they know how. When are those who make it out of the ghetto going to start giving back to their community? Just like you can't raise a child by throwing the baby-momma money and running off and not being with the child, the same goes to those who give money but don't show their faces. We need more physical bodies in the community to guide our young Black men. They need to be taught how to be a man by example, by how we live, by physically being there, seeing our actions, not just giving monetary donations. This is especially true when a young man's Father, Uncle or Grandpop is either dead, locked up or messed up and lost himself. Other than that, you already know how this story goes, but you don't know how it's going to end.

Kino comes back from the store getting some eggs and milk for his Mother.

"Yall hold on, let me put this up in the house." He goes into the house and puts the groceries in the kitchen. For some reason he kisses his Mother and tells her "I love you Ma." She smiles and watches him walk out the door wondering what he's up to. He walks over to Poochy and Murk then says, "This what we going to do"... - he pauses then says - "We gonna get this money to get Coupe out."

CHAPTER TWENTY-FOUR

Kino and Poochy go to work. Before they clock in, Poochy asks Kino, "When we going back on the block? I'm ready to walk out this spot now."

Kino recollects his Pop's words. "My Pop said to always keep it real. Mr. Clydell kept it real to us and gave us another chance, so we gonna keep it real to him."

"So we not gonna quit?" asks Poochy.

"Yeah, but with a two-week notice. You don't remember knucklehead, that all he asked for was us to not do another no show? So if we quit, we give him a two-week notice; we owe him that much. If a cracker was our manager you know our ass woulda been fired and wouldn't have been able to come back.

"Yeah, you right bra," Poochy says.

They walk into Mr. Clydell's office.

"What's up Mr. Clydell?" Kino and Poochy say.

"What's going on?" he replies.

Kino and Poochy look at each other, both wondering who's going to speak.

"This is our two-week notice," Poochy blurts out.

"Sir, we trying to give you the respect that you deserve for giving us a second chance. So we giving you a two-week notice instead of walking out on you," Kino says.

"I appreciate yall for respecting me, but the two-week notice is for your benefit. The respect should also be for your co-workers, not only me," Mr. Clydell told them.

"How is giving you a two-week notice a benefit to us? And what does it have to do with my co-workers?" asks Kino.

"When you apply for another job, you can always use McDonalds as a reference, showing that you have experience and are a responsible worker. When you quit any job and don't give a two-week notice, then try to use that job as a reference, you will look bad to the company thinking of hiring you. As for your co-workers, just think when a person shows up late or doesn't show up at all, look at how you have to pick up their load and work two jobs and longer hours. By you giving the managers a two-week notice, that gives us time to hire someone else and replace you before you leave. This is how you will get a good reference versus walking out and getting a bad reference. That's why it's for you.

"I never thought about it that way," Poochy says.

"So why yall quitting?" asks Mr. Clydell.

They look at each other again. If these jits think they can fool this veteran old G., who got out the game but can still recognize game, then they are either crazy or dumb. Kino's embarrassed to tell the truth (even though it's eating him up inside). He feels bad to mention he's getting back in the game because he bragged to Mr. Clydell about his father's words.

"Poochy 's father is sick and my Mother is in the hospital," Kino blurts out. Mr. Clydell already knows that what Kino said is bullshit. He started to question them more just to make them look stupid. Instead he respected them for the fact that they at least came and gave him a two-week notice. He told them, "Yall just remember what I told you about them streets. Because you gave me a two-week notice, you're always welcome back here, and I'll give you a good reference if you try to get another job somewhere else."

They dap Mr. Clydell and tell him thanks, then went to clock in and start working.

CHAPTER TWENTY-FIVE

"Diane Ford is a thirty-three-year-old White female from Washington D.C. She's the owner of the credit card found in the car registered to Curtis Placky," said the secretary of the Metro Bureau of Investigation's office in Orlando.

"Is that all?" M.B.I. Agent Byron McMill asks.

"The credit card was reported stolen at the West Gate Resort on International Drive, across the street from the club where the murders took place Sunday night. It was a robbery, a purse snatching," she said.

"Can Ms. Ford identify Placky as the robber?" asks Agent Byron.

"In the police report she says she didn't see who it was. He had a mask or a shirt tied over his face."

"Get me her phone number, I'm going to call her."

"Yes sir," answered the secretary.

"Did we get the results of the bullet casings found at the scene of the murdered dogs?"

"No, not yet. The lab tech is waiting on some parts being shipped from overseas for the equipment to work."

"So that's the same for the bullet found in the back seat of Placky's car?" asks the agent.

"Yes sir, the lab tech said as soon as the parts come in and the machine is fixed he will examine both the casing and the bullet."

"Are there any known relations between Placky and Giovoni?" "Placky's name was never mentioned in any paperwork or briefs."

"Call our informant and set up a meeting. I have questions for him."

"Yes sir, Agent Byron."

CHAPTER TWENTY-SIX

Murk is still on the block, trapped in a vicious cycle, which is why he cannot come up. He's like a cat chasing its tail, spinning in circles. He buys dope to flip on the block, sells it, then takes all the profit and get high and drunk, leaving him right back with the same amount he started with. Sometimes he gambles while he's high and drunk, playing Tunk, Skinn, or shooting dice. Gambling or snorting his re-up money away, leaving him dead ass broke. Somehow he manages to borrow ten dollars and buys a big dime from DoeBoy. He flips that big dime to a couple of hundred dollars. That's when he goes back to snorting, drinking and gambling until he's back broke. He goes from one dope boy to another. Back and forth between DoeBoy and Mango who sells snorting powder. From hustling to snorting powder all night until the next morning, this is the cycle Murk lives every day.

Kino comes home from school and Murk's knocked out.
He looks at Murk flopped on the bed with his sneakers on, fully dressed, smelling like cigarettes and alcohol. Slob's coming out of his mouth, looking like he just went to sleep.

"Murk! ... Murk! Wake up!" Kino taps and shakes him.
"What man?" Murk says in a cranky voice.
"Let me get some money so I can get some dope and start getting this money for Coupe."

"I ain't got no money."

"What? How in the hell? You been hustling all these weeks and you dead ass broke?" Kino walks out the room and calls Poochy.

- phone ringing -

"What's up bra bra?" answers Poochy.

"You got any money bra? Murk done drunk, smoked and snorted all his money, he dead-ass broke."

"Nah bra, I gave my last check to Mom and she still talking about the lights might be getting cut off."

"Well we got to wait until we get paid from McDonalds before we can start," Kino says.

"Aight," Poochy says, "I'll meet you at McDonalds in the morning. I'll holla at ya then."

"Aight bra," Kino tells him, then hangs up and goes back to the room where Murk's at and wakes him up.

"What you want bro? Can't you see I'm trying to sleep?"

"Nigga, your ass don't deserve the sleep. You don't pay no bills, you still eating all the food in the house, but you ain't putting nothing in the cabinets, broke-ass nigga."

"Call me that again and I'm a beat your ass bra."

"Broke-ass nigga," Kino yells at Murk.

Murk jumped out the bed at Kino, but before he could get halfway up, Kino hit him with a straight right sending Murk on his ass. Usually it's a good fight between them two, but Murk is weak, tired and still intoxicated. His reflexes are slower. He tries to get up but he feels the fight is out of him. He lost this battle mentally and physically.

Murk sits back down with his back against the wall. His head is down. He makes no sobbing sound. He does not even look like he's humbling himself, but Kino senses that he is. Murk is too quiet and not trying to attack Kino. He lifts his head up and looks at Kino right in the eyes and yells - "Nobody loves me! Nobody cares!" All Kino sees are tears running down Murk's face. You ever see a grown man cry where his cry is noiseless, without emotions, only tears stream down the cheekbones from the eyes. Kino walks over to him and bends down to hug him, but Murk pushes him off. Murk stands up and Kino grabs him again. They wrestle a bit back and forth. But each time Murk resists a bit less, then Kino yells "I love you bro! I love you bro!" Finally, Murk hugs Kino back and says, "I love you too bro."

Kino tells Murk, "I love ya, Mama loves ya, Precious loves ya, we all love ya bra. You got to be strong Murk. We got to help Ma out. We got to get Coupe out. You got to look after your sister. How you going to do any of this getting high every day, blowing all your money? You might as well be smoking the dope, and I know you ain't no baser!"

"Hell no!" Murk replied.

"Then stop acting like one," Kino told him. Murk gave Kino some dap and said, "You're right bro."

"Now, take your ass back to sleep, or go brush your teeth, because your breath stank as hell," Kino told Murk. Murk punched Kino in the arm and Kino ran as they both laughed.

****

Friday morning Kino and Poochy skip school and meet at McDonalds. They pick up their checks and catch the bus to Food Mart to get their checks cashed. They run into some homies they know from the Pork-n-Bean Projects on Ivey Lane, when they went to Ivey Lane Elementary.

"Bird, that's you?" Kino asks.

"What's up Kino? What you up to?" he asks as they give each other dap and hug.

"Me and Poochy cashing our checks and getting ready to burn the block up."

"Toedoe outside in the car. We fin' to go post-up at Big B's and get this paper." Poochy comes out the bathroom and sees Bird.

"What's up Bird?" Poochy yells and gives him play and a hug. "Bra bra, what it be?" replied Bird.

They walk out of the store to Bird's car and Toedoe sees them and jumps out of the car to meet and greet Kino and Poochy.

"Damn bra, you rolling like this?" Poochy asks.

Bird is driving a box Chevy on twenty sixes, regular clean paint, no music, no guts (interior). He only has the twenty sixes.

"Ain't yall supposed to be at Jones High?" Kino asks them.

"Ain't yall supposed to be at Evans High?" Toedoe replies back as they all laugh.

"Poochy, I heard you moved to Apopka. You go to Apopka High?" asks Bird.

"I represent A.P.K. to the fullest bra, but I go to E. High."

"Where Coupe and Murk at?" asks Toedoe.

"Murk was a bad motherfucker in school. He use to cuss the teachers out every day and kept us fighting them niggas from Mercy Drive," says Bird.

"Where his twin sister at?" asks Toedoe.

"You did have a crush on her," Kino says to Toedoe.

"Murk moved in with me and my Mom when he came home from prison. We stay on Mercy Drive now."

"What about Coupe?   What's up with him?" Bird asks.

"Coupe locked up for attempted murder and cruelty to animals," Kino told them.

"Damn, that's fucked up," Toedoe says.

"We trying to get him out now. Ten stacks for his bond."

Bird looks at Toedoe then Toedoe says, "Count us for a stack towards his bond. I got five hundred, you got five Bird?"

"Damn right I got it. That nigga use to make us laugh even though he was scary as hell, he still our homie."

"He ain't scary no more," Poochy says. "I got into it in the Palms with some niggas and Coupe was slapping them niggas with a stick getting them off me," Poochy says.

"Damn bra, it be about a hundred niggas in the Palms. How yall get out of that? You being from Apopka and didn't

Coupe move to Pinehills?" asks Bird.

"We were with Murk. Him and Kino live on the drive. So nobody really jumped in but a couple of the homies of the nigga I was fighting. Everybody else watched. Plus, everybody knew the nigga I was fighting was messing up the money on the block with that fuck-shit. Coupe stood in the paint for me and didn't run."

"I had to beat a nigga ass the other day for snatching a jug's money and running off. I told him don't do that fuck-shit around here. Shoot, he messing up the money," says Toedoe.

"We need to get some work. When we flip it a couple of times, we'll get that bread to ya," Bird says.

"We going to get some work too, in the Palms," Poochy says. "They say they got whatever you want in the Palms; big dimes, fifty packs, balls, cookies, ounces of soft, four ways, quarters whatever you want. We both trying to spend like two grand a piece," says Bird.

"Give us a ride to the Palms and we got ya. We know everybody that got work there," says Kino.

They get into the Chevy and head to Mercy Drive. On the way, Kino tells them, "DoeBoy got nothing but iron, but he don't sell cookies, only balls, packs, big dimes and nicks. T sells cookies, but he be having that water."

"Who got the ounces in powder? We can pay this jug to cook it for us. Them niggas be getting over on us selling it to us cooked up," Bird tells Kino and Poochy.

Kino takes Bird to Dolly who sells weight in powder and tells him to get Toedoe's money, because he doesn't want to spook Dolly by bringing more than one person.

- knocking on Dolly's door –
"Who is it?"
"It's me Dolly, Kino."
He opens the door with a long barrel chrome 357 in his hand. He looks at Kino, then Bird.

"Who dat?"

"My homie. I brought him to get some work."

"You the police bra?" asks Dolly.

"Nah bra, I'm from the Bean, Ivey Lane."

Dolly moves out the doorway and lets them in. He then closes the door and locks it. He puts the pistol back in his waist.

"What you want jit?"

"I got four grand," Bird says.

"Ounces, seven fifty, eighths are thirty-one fifty. You can get an eighth and one ounce," Dolly tells him.

"Cooking dope not no snorting dope," Bird says.

"I don't sell no bullshit man."

Dolly goes to the room and comes back out with two sandwich bags of dope. One bag is the ounce and the other one is the eighth. Kino never saw cocaine powder before.

"Damn, that looks like fish scale," Kino says.

Bird looks at the dope and sees the pearl color all through the dope as it's compressed in layers of flakes.

Bird gives Dolly the money, then they leave. Bird puts the dope up in the car. He and Kino talk in the breezeway.

"Where Toedoe and Poochy went?" asks Bird.

"They probably went to go get Murk, we stay across the street in Peppertree. How much are you going to make off that?" asks Kino.

"I got five and a half ounces. Off of one ounce I can drop three cookies, ten, nine, and nine grams a piece. I can sell those for three fifty to four hundred a piece, according to who buys it. Let's just say at three fifty a piece, I'll make a thousand and fifty dollars off each ounce. Off these five and a half ounces, I'll make around fifty-eight hundred. And that's just serving cookies. I paid thirty-nine hundred and make almost a two grand profit in selling weight. If I was to get off this dope in weight over there at Big B's, I could sell out in a hour or two. But me and Toedoe is going to grind all this dope. Them niggas don't really got no weight man over there. So we grind all ours out we ain't selling them nothing. I'm a get this jug name Lucky, pay him a hundred dollars and throw him a fifty pack and let him cook it all up. Kino, when we grind this out, we'll make around ten grand."

Kino's mind went to thinking so he asks him, "How long will it take for you to grind it all out?"

"One day, on the right day, two days on an average, three to four when it's slow and we bullshitting."

"But if you was to sell it in weight, it could be gone in a hour?" asks Kino.

"Less than that when it's bumpin'. One time I brought an ounce for eight hundred and cut eleven big balls off it. I sold it to all the hustlers in balls. I was out in ten minutes, and had eleven hundred dollars. I couldn't get no more dope. My connect was out, that's why I paid that high price from someone else and my power jugs was hitting me up for two and three hundred dollar sales. I coulda grinded that dope and made over two grand, but I sold it in weight and was out for the rest of the day. Bra, my phone was blowing up all night. I had to turn it off. A nigga I sold three balls to, I sold most of his dope for him, just to keep my clientele coming. I told them niggas, never again. I'm a grind all my dope. So if you ever get a hold of some weight, come sit with me at Big B's and I'll help you get off all it."

Poochy, Toedoe and Murk come back to the breezeway where Kino and Bird are talking. Murk and Bird rush to each other, give each other play, then hug each other.

"What's up bra?   I heard you did a bid. I see you got your weight up," Bird tells Murk.

"You still a lady's man, messing with everybody's girlfriend, having us fighting some other click every day because you done took someone's girlfriend?" They all started laughing when Murk said that.

"Look, Kino got my number, hit me up. You see, I'm

rolling on twenty sixes, haha. I'll come scoop yall up," Bird says.

"Nigga, you ain't got no drop in there," Murk says.

"Not yet, just wait, coming soon candy paint and all. Come on Toedoe, we got to find Lucky and rent Mama Lisa's kitchen out, then get this money. "

"The first money we make going towards freeing Coupe my nigga," said Toedoe.

"Damn right my nigga. Free Coupe!" Bird yelled out as he cranked up his Chevy, making them pipes holla, pumping the gas pedal.

Kino and Poochy go to the back and holla at DoeBoy and buy a ball a piece. Their check was only a hundred and thirty dollars each. Each time they sold out, they went right back to DoeBoy. By the time night fell, they had over five hundred a piece. Kino hadn't seen any of his jugs. He wanted to wait until he got up to a stack before he called them. They both spent five hundred a piece, then burned the block until they sold out. It was about two in the morning and they had been out there since yesterday morning. Kino and Poochy take it in. Poochy spends the night at Kino's house. Murk gives his money to Kino and only takes a hundred dollars with him and goes to the party house with Mont the knockout king.

The party house is a five-minute walk from The Palms in a house in one of the neighborhoods located off Mercy Drive. You know what's going down at the party house. Cocaine snorting and tricking-ass hoes. All the old G's and the shot callers from the Drive who party hang out there. A party house full of niggas with a mouth full of gold, bald heads and crazy dreads, drunk and skeeted up on cocaine partying all night, and I'm not talking about music and dancing partying. I'm talking about snorting all night partying. That's why it's called the party house.

CHAPTER TWENTY-SEVEN

In a small three-bedroom apartment in the projects called Beirut is where Tanisha lives with her Mother, little sister, and her daughter. Recently her Aunt moved in with her two kids.

Shawana stays in the next building over with her Mother and three brothers, two older than her and one younger than Shawana. The oldest one, Micky, smokes crack and steals from everybody, including their Mother. Next to the oldest is her brother Paul, who is a straight book geek. He stays away from the dope game, but he's a stone cold freak. Her younger brother Toot thinks he's in the game, but cannot manage to come up - he's more of a fuck-up.

Tanisha and Shawana are at Carver Court Park across the street with Khadeejah, Tanisha's daughter and her little sister Kenyatta.

"You talked to Kino lately?" asks Shawana.

"Yes, he calls me every day, even just to say hi and ask me how am I doing."

"Poochy haven't called me in a couple of days."

"Why you won't call him?" asks Tanisha.

"Because I got to make sure he wants me before I give it to him and not just want my snap back pussy."

"Child please, more like that loose ocean down there you have. How you snapping or gripping on anything. You got to stop having sex so it could tighten up. And if you do, don't let no big dick Willie jump up and down in you, banging your insides out, because if you don't marry that person all the other men you run across will get lost in your beat up pussy and drown," she says laughing.

"I ain't got to worry about that," Shawana says.

"I can't tell, not the way they talking about you," Tanisha says.

"So when was the last time you had sex, Ms. Goody Two Shoes Tanisha?"

"A year ago, and it was with my baby daddy," Tanisha looks at Shawana already knowing the answer and asks anyway. "And you?"

Shawana turns her head and says, "Don't worry about that, let's just say I'm saving this for Poochy and I'm ready to give it to him. I just don't want him to be like all the other men I have given it to."

"What about all the other men?" Tanisha asks.

Either I find out they got a lady, they don't call back, or all they call me for is to have sex, or their dick is just plain sorry. You remember Mike?" asks Shawana.

"The one with the big lips and had a lot of money?"

"Yea. Girl, his breath was stank. He gave me no foreplay. He just got on top of me and started humping like a jack rabbit, pounded me hard for one minute, nutted, then rolled over like he done something."

Tanisha cracked up laughing and said, "That's what you get for always giving your pussy up so fast."

"Well, when you going to give Kino some?"

"When the time is right," Tanisha says.

"You still ain't tell me when," Shawana replies.

"Why you want to know so bad?"

"Because I don't know when the right time is for me to give it to Poochy and I want to fuck him now."

"Girl, you wanted to fuck him the first night in the club," Shawana pushes Tanisha, and they both laugh.

"No, serious Tanisha, I like him and I don't want to mess this one up."

"Make that nigga wait. If he likes you for you, then he'll stay around. If he just wants to fuck and you don't give it to him, then he'll leave. You got to be stronger than him and hold out if you really want to know if he likes you or not, or he just wants to fuck."

"I don't know what I'm going to do," Shawana says, like she's getting ready to explode and fuck the next thing that's walking and has a dick.

"Girl, you need to pray. Pray to God for strength and keep your legs closed. That's how I do it," Tanisha tells her.

"Yeah, because one year I woulda been broke my finger!" Shawana says, as they both start laughing.

The Messenger of Allah, peace and blessings be upon him, said (paraphrasing): *"One of the signs of the last day is that there will be a decrease of religious knowledge (teachings) and an increase of ignorance."* If you contemplate on that hadith, you will see how true it is. Just think about it. According to religion - A PERSON IS NOT SUPPOSE TO HAVE SEX UNTIL THEY GET MARRIED. The Prophet Muhammad, peace and blessings be upon him, said "There will be a decrease in religious knowledge and an increase of ignorance."

If people are not being taught, led, or guided by the knowledge of the Creator, then they're being taught, led or guided by ignorance, and their own desires. The opposite of knowledge is ignorance, and if it is not the knowledge from your Creator, then it is ignorance.

Just ask yourself, whoever's reading this book, "Do I TEACH my child to abstain from sex until they get married?" I did say TEACH and not TELL, because there is a difference between teaching and telling. Anybody can tell you something, but as parents we should be teaching, not telling. Teaching entails communicating with your child and communicating is explaining to then by educating them on the consequences of diseases, having bastard children, dealing with different baby daddy's or baby mommas, versus dealing with only one who they truly love and are married to. Explain to them how it's so much better to have all your children grow up together in the same house versus having children spread out not knowing each other. The best way to teach your child is by example. What do you look like if you teach your child to be chaste until they marry, but yet they see you in an intimate relationship with someone who you're not married to?

That's not an example. For those who say they TELL their children to wait until marriage, that is not an efficient way to raise a child. You have to teach them. And if you do not have any children, ask yourself were you taught, not told, by your parents to wait until you get married? Back in the days, and I mean way back, it would be normal to find a virgin for marriage. You would find a woman with eight, nine, ten and even fifteen children all by one man, her husband. You would be frowned upon to be a bastard child. Nowadays just about everybody I know is a bastard and most people have bastard children. People have no shame of that anymore. This is the result of a decrease in religious knowledge.

Shawana has no example teaching her because all her siblings have different Fathers. Her Mother has never been married. She is guided by the increase of ignorance following her desires. And this is the same reason why Tanisha has a baby daddy who she can't stand. So what are you going to do to become better and TEACH your children to be better?

CHAPTER TWENTY-EIGHT

Mama Lisa is a veteran hoodrat in her mid-thirties. Five kids, five different baby-daddies. Government subsidies pay her bills. Across the street from Big B's is Lake Man Garden Apartments where Mama Lisa pays twenty-five dollars a month as a HUD resident. She's the same woman but looks different every week, with a different hairstyle, different hair color, with matching fingernails and clothes. She likes young niggas like Monique. They don't have to have money like Monique only be able to blow her back out and buy her some weed to smoke.

- knock knock -

"Who is it?" Mama Lisa screams while she's poppin' and chewing bubble gum.
"Bird and Toedoe, girl."
Mama Lisa yells to her son, "Jermaine, open the door!" Her five-year-old boy gets up from playing the Play Station and opens the door. As soon as they walk in they get shot with a water gun from two of her older sons, eight and ten years of age. Bird puts the box he's carrying down and chases one of them and Toedoe chases the other one. Toys and clothes are scattered everywhere. It looks like a kids' bedroom after a sleepover that took place in their living room. Mama Lisa's sister has four kids of her own. She stays in the same building. Sometimes all of them are over at Mama Lisa's house when their Mother goes out tricking.

Bird trips over some Lego toys and falls. The five-year-old throws his Incredible Hulk toy right at Bird's head. Bem!! It landed perfect, right on the side of his head. "Leave my brother alone," he screamed. Toedoe bursts out laughing at Bird. That's when the two older brothers sprayed Toedoe again with water. The smoker Lucky comes in through the door and rushes the two jits and says, "Not this time, yall got me before, but not today." He grabs one of them, Toedoe grabs the other one, and Bird gets up and grabs the little five-year-old. They put each one of them in a headlock, make a fist and start mauling their heads with their hands, rubbing back and forth with their fists real fast, applying pressure to their heads. Bird, Toedoe and Lucky are laughing their asses off saying, "Who's laughing now?" Not these bad Bae Bae kids, they mad as hell.

They start crying and swinging like a windmill trying to fight Bird and them. Mama Lisa comes out of her room and yells, "What in da' hell yall doing?"

"They started it Mom," they say, while they're sobbing. These kids shift gears from laughing to crying to being furiously mad in three seconds. "Get in your room, all of yall," Mama Lisa yells at them. The two older ones walk to their room cussing, shooting Toedoe and them birds with their middle fingers. The little five-year-old had to get one in before he left, so he ran and kicked Bird and grunted, "umm!" as he kicked.

Mama Lisa said, "Boy!" then popped him hard as hell with her hand straight to his forehead - "Pop!" - is sounded off. "Get in your room!" she yelled. He bust out crying loud as hell and ran full speed into his room and slammed the door behind him. "Shut that mouth up boy before I come in there with my belt." All you hear is another grunt - "umm! " - as he kicked the door.

Mama Lisa turned to Bird and Toedoe and said, "Where my money and weed?" Bird gives her fifty dollars and Toedoe gives her an ounce of regular good weed. They go in the kitchen and pay Lucky.

Bird gives him the box with the bowls, scale, bags and baking soda. Toedoe gives him the dope. Mama Lisa goes back in her room. Lucky does not allow Bird and Toedoe watch him cook. He makes them get out the kitchen. That's how he eats and he told them "Get out, the game is made to be sold, not showed." Bird and Toedoe go to the Bae Bae kids' bedroom and open the door. Bird asks them, "Why yall trippin'? Yall started it first." One of them said, "Mommy's boyfriends always be beating on us, so my Daddy said to attack every man that comes in the house." Bird said, "Look buddy, we yall partners. If any man puts their hands on yall, call me and we'll come handle them for yall." Toedoe pulls out some money and gives each one of them twenty dollars. They run and hug Toedoe and Bird. Bird grabs the little one and takes his own shirt and wipes his snotty nose and wet face from tears, hugs him, and says "Yall be good." Toedoe gives them their number, then they leave and yell, "Lucky, call us when you're almost through."

CHAPTER TWENTY-NINE

Two weeks from turning eighteen, still a teenager, charged with a case that could keep him incarcerated until his mid forty's, basically a life sentence. What's sad about this situation is that Coupe is innocent of these crimes. The system does not understand a Black Man's situation, but the people who run the system surely do. Three elements determine what is right and wrong, guilty or innocent in today's legal system: money, power or relations. Coupe as well as the average Black Man in America has none of these elements to free themselves from this modern day slavery called prison.

His only hope is money, because he knows no one in power, meaning a judge, lawyer, politician, or someone in a high office working for the government. He definitely has no power himself. Coupe's compadres are his only hope.

Orange County Jail in Orlando, Florida classifies inmates by the color of your armband. white being the lowest of security. With a white armband you can work outside of the jail and be on the road crew. These are misdemeanor charges with around thirty-day jail sentences. When the inmates see a person in the Orange County Jail with a white armband, they tell that person, "you got a Rolex on." The red armbands are usually no bond or high bond status, more violent felony charges like murder, attempted murder, home invasion, kidnapping, armed robbery, etc. All of these inmates are in the same cell, being monitored by heavy security.

They place Coupe on the fifth floor with a red armband. Anxiety runs through Coupe's body as he enters the dorm on the fifth floor of the main building. Each dorm consists of four cells. The dayroom consists of two phone, two tables, one T.V. and an open shower with two sprayers. Not only do these inmates look different than the ones he was with at Central Booking, but the intensity, demeanor, vibe or feeling in this part of the jail is totally on a different level. A scary level having Coupe feeling like a hamster in a cage of snakes, and he better not blink or all hell will break loose. All these inmates are looking at twenty years to life. The time they're looking at is long and their charges are egregious. Most of them, if not all of them, in this dorm are seasoned vets. They had been to prison before, killed before, kidnapped people, robbed, been shot or shot at before. They probably have no family support. All friends, girlfriends or wives have turned their backs on them, leaving them for dead. They live off the land, or should I say, screwing over each other is part of survival in the streets and definitely in prison. This is the environment this innocent young man walks into. Scared as hell. Coupe has never been locked up before. He walks into the dorm and sees niggas big as hell, looking like they came out their Mamma's pussy doing push-ups.

Niggas are arguing at the table over whose hood makes more money. One of them says, "Nigga, I got plenty of money, I'm a trailblazer. Millions of dollars on the Trail. You got 18th Street, 29th Street, 39th Street, like five different hotels jumping, even the Parliament House nigga, the whole Trail from Colonial to the Florida Mall, ain't none of us broke."

The other nigga is yelling, "Cross town nigga. All up Westmoreland from West 50 all the way down to 29th. Then you got Federal, Livingston, Polk Street, Garden, Paramore. Nigga I be on South Street, Divisions, Griffin Park, Jackson, Beirut, Quill Street. Niggas Cross town we make millions of dollars. I don't know what you talking about. We ain't broke."

Coupe carries his box upstairs into his cell where inmates are playing Tunk for push-ups.

"Caught your ass nigga, give me double."

"Shit!" the other man says.

"Get down and give me forty."

Both of them have their shirts off and look like they've been pumpin' helium in their arms and chests. One of the old G's is sitting on his bunk and says to Coupe, "What's up youngsta? That's your bunk on top, right there," The cell is built for four inmates but Orange County added four more beds to each cell and put beds in the dayroom. Everybody is cramped up like sardines creating an even more hostile environment.

"My name Boogy. Where you from jit?" the old G asks.

"Pinehills," Coupe tells him, in a squeaky voice.

"Here goes a toothbrush and toothpaste. Big Ant, give him some toilet paper and soap," he tells Ant.

"Let me bust Mouse ass up again, then I'll get it."

"The only thing you fin' to bust up nigga is this floor," Mouse says, as he drops, "twenty-eight."

"Nigga, you tried me after three pulls," Big Ant says as he throws the cards down mad as hell, because he got twenty-nine.

"I'm watching you. You ain't switch nah card, plus you throwing out seven and eights," Mouse says.

"Nigga, I'm trying to Tunk on your ass." Big Ant gets even more furious when he checks the next two cards in the deck because of curiosity to see what his pull was if Mouse didn't drop, and low and behold it was his spread card. When he pulled it, he slammed it down and said, "Damn!" Everybody starts laughing.

"Get your ass down nigga!" This laugh eased Coupe's soul for the seconds the laugh lasts. The niggas that was in the dayroom are now yelling and cussing each other out. The stupid thing about their whole argument is that they're arguing about other niggas who have money from their hood. Both of them are broke as hell. They are arguing about another man's money.

"You talking all that shit, nigga we can go in the room."

"Fuck you nigga, what you waiting for?"

Both of them run upstairs and go into the cell next to Coupe's cell. Big Ant, Mouse, and Boogy walk out of their cell, but only Big Ant walks into the cell where they're fighting. He's from Polk Street so he walks into the cell where they're fighting and says "Ain't nobody fin' to jump my boy!" Big Ant and others in the cell slide the beds over while the two belligerent men strap up their sneakers, then go at it. Coupe is trying to see the fight, but Boogy grabs him and says, "Come on," and leads him back in their cell. Another nigga comes out of the cell they're fighting in and tells everybody in the dorm to go back in their cells and act normal. Coupe sees two correctional officers walk by the dorm talking. He shakes his head and says to himself, "Damn these niggas in here trying to kill each other and everybody's standing around like nothing is going on, while the officers walk by gossiping to each other."

CHAPTER THIRTY

Riviera Apartments is where Dirty Red and his homies stay. It's off Mercy Drive, a five-minute walk to the Palms Apartments. Mercy Drive is one street in Orlando that consists of eight different apartment complexes and about three neighborhoods of houses. The Palms Apartments is the center of attraction. Everybody from Mercy Drive hustles or hangs out at The Palms. A lot of Pinehills niggas are there too. Because Pinehills use to be the place where, when your parents got a better job and more money, they would move to for a better and safer living. It was terribly boring in Pinehills. Mostly middle-class White people. Those of us who moved to Pinehills would hang out and hustle on Mercy Drive. That's why a lot of Mercy Drive niggas back in the days are also from Pinehills. Nowadays, Pinehills is just or even more off the chain as Mercy Drive, and has turned all Black. All the White people left. Pinehills is now called Crime Hills.

Dirty Red and his crew are in Riviera Shores walking to The Palms Apartments.

"That nigga Kino is locking down all the power jugs. I haven't seen Big Money Charley or the trick who comes in the Benzs," says Dirty Red.

"They say Kino giving them jugs extra dope, fucking up the game and he the one who got Poochy and Coupe over there. Them niggas ain't even from the Drive," one of his partners says, a guy who jumped in when Dirty Red was fighting Poochy. Dirty Red made a suggestion, then says, "We going to start telling niggas Kino is the police."

"That nigga Coupe locked up on attempted murder charges."
"That's perfect, we can start telling people Kino got him jammed up," Dirty Red says.

They get to The Palms and see Kino, Poochy, and Murk on the block hustling. They walk to the back and holla at Doeboy, re-up and start serving.

"Ain't that Dirty Red and them niggas?" Kino asks.

"Them niggas don't want no action," Murk says.

"I ain't worried about them doing nothing physical, I just don't trust them. I got a bad feeling about them," Kino says.

"It ain't nothing for me to knock that nigga out again," Poochy says.

"Just watch them niggas. I'm fin' to ride with Becky and get this money," Kino says.

"Nah, you fin' to fuck Becky nigga. I know you tricking these jugs," Murk says laughing.

Becky pulls up in a brand new Benz. Kino gets in and they pull out. She takes him straight to the Parliament House on Orange Blossom Trail, a motel exclusively for homosexuals, lesbians, and B.D.S.M. people, which means Bondage, Discipline, Sadism and Masochism. Never has Kino seen weirder Black and White people in his life. He thought he was at a circus that exposed the weirdest people on earth. The first strange person he noticed was a five foot six, three-hundred-pound man in pink biker shorts with spiked hair. His socks were pulled up to his knees and he walked with a twist, holding hands with a six foot two, hundred and fifty-pound man. Murk follows Becky into the lobby and sees one of the baddest bitches he ever saw in his life. She's thick-to-death and has a booty you can put a drink on. She's dressed jazzy as hell in high heels with a mini skirt revealing her hour glass shape. She has long, beautiful, Black hair. Kino is stuck in a trance, staring at her from behind. He says to himself, "Damn, what the hell she doing here?"

"Jazzabell!" someone calls her name and she turns around and shocks the hell out of Kino. You would've thought he saw a ghost. He saw a diamond silver face, and I'm not talking about a ten piece in looks diamond, I'm talking about real diamond earrings piercing all in her face. She had one in each nostril, one on each eyebrow, three at the bottom of her lip and one on the side of each cheek. Then she had six in each ear, on top of tattoos on her face, and one piercing on her tongue. Kino looks at the woman calling her. He shook his head as this amazon body building woman, taller than Kino, standing six three, walks by Kino to hug and kiss her. Kino turns to Becky and says, "Where in the hell you got me at?"

"You just hope you have enough dope," she tells him.

They go into the room and an old White man in his fifties is there. He's drinking a bottle of Johnny Walker Blue and says, "What's up?" Kino says, "What's up?" back. Becky kisses the old White dude and says, "George, this Kino who I was telling you about." George has a double room connected by one door in the back.

"Where Robin and Bob at?" asks Becky.

"In the other room smoking," George tells Becky. She strips off all her clothes in front of Kino and George.

"Kino, have a hundred ready when I get through," Becky told him, as she took out a gym bag and started pulling out all sorts of toys.

Little does Kino know that Becky is part of the B.D.S.M. community. Sadism is pleasure derived from causing pain, and masochism is pleasure derived from being subjected to pain or humiliation. And sadomasochism is one who enjoys both the pleasure from inflicting pain on others and being subjected to abuse and domination.

Becky was a madam at an upscale exclusive brothel who became addicted to smoking crack cocaine. She left the brothel and took some customers with her. Blonde hair, green eyes, flat booty, big breasted and chalky white creamy skin was her make up. She could hold a conversation with senators or kick it in the hood. Her face looks like her prettiness is dwindling away from her because of drug use. She was Ms. Florida at one time in her life, with a Master's Degree in Business. Now she's a sadomasochist who smokes dope and prostitute's big money clients. Her client George is a real estate mogul who is a masochist. They met at the brothel.

The first thing she pulled out was a Black leather skirt and a Black leather bustier. She then pulled out a bullwhip, paddles, ropes and a Black leather wrist and ankle restraints. She stood out in front of George and shook her big breasted titties, spun around and said, "Take one last look boy," then cracked the whip on his chest and said, "Cover your eyes." His face turned red as hell and Kino said, "Ouch!" when the whip landed on him.

George took both of his hands and covered his eyes and face then turned around. Becky then quickly put on her leather skirt and bustier. Wearing no panties, she stepped into some high heels. She told Kino that George gets a thrill from other people watching him get abused and humiliated. She cracked the whip again on his back, then told him to turn around and said, "you can look now." He turned around and gawked her up and down as she was looking like the Cat Woman, half naked. Then Becky ran and jumped into his arms and they violently kissed as she ripped his five hundred dollar Giorgio Armani button up collar dress shirt off. She pushed him on the bed and forcefully snatched his buttons loose on his Armani trousers. She then steps back and tells George to strip everything off. Kino started to leave and said, "Hell no, I ain't with this kinky freaky shit." George begged Kino to watch.

"Please don't go," his submissive voice spoke. "I'll pay you extra money if he stays," he told Becky.

Becky looked at Kino and said, "If you want this money honey, then stay for the show." She smiled a creepy smile then cracked that bullwhip right smack on George's leg then said to him, "Shut up!" He jumped and yelled, "Yes honey! Come on baby, paddle me, please paddle me."

Becky commanded him, "Get on the floor you dog. On all fours." She got the paddle and started whooping him with the paddle. Kino couldn't take it anymore when she got on top of him and gave him a golden shower. Kino hauled ass out of that room and went into the other room where Robin and Bob were. Robin had a collar around her neck and was chained to a strip pole. Bob was hitting the pipe smoking crack while Robin was giving him a blowjob. Kino said "I had enough of this," and left out of the room and went to the lobby. He walked around and explored the club and restaurant at the motel.

CHAPTER THIRTY-ONE

Dirty Red sold all his dope on the block, so he tells his click, "I'm fin' to go re-up and holla at Doeboy."

"We going to the store to get some wings and fries," Red's homies say.

On the way to Doeboy's, Dirty Red sees T who sells the water cookies.

"What up T?"

"What's up Dirty Red? What's going on?"

"I'll tell you what's up. Don't trust that nigga Kino, I think he's the police."

"Why you say that bra?" T asks.

"I seen him in the back of Pettertree one night talking with the po'pos. The same Duke Boys who arrested Poochy, now he's out of jail. They say Coupe and Kino got into it so he set up the police to pull Coupe over and told them crackers about some murders Coupe and Murk did. He didn't tell on Murk, just Coupe."

"Oh yeah? I knew it was something about that nigga," T says.

"I'm just trying to look out for my homies. Mercy Drive nigga!"

They gave each other dap and T goes to Dolly who serves the weight in powder to tell him.

- T knocking on Dolly's door -

"Who is it?"

"This T fool."

Dolly opens the door with that same old school chrome long barrel 357 in his hand. He opens the door and let's T in.

"What's up bra?" T asks.

162

"I only got one block left and I'm fin' to bag this up in eighths and quarters."

"Nah bra, I'm straight for now, but I will be ready tomorrow."

"I'm waiting on Giovoni now, you know how that goes, you never know when he's coming. He never lets you know when its in."

"Bra, I really came to talk to you about Kino."

"That jit from Peppertree, crazy-ass Murk's brother?"

"Yeah, they say he's the police," T says.

"That nigga brought some dude to buy some work from me the other day."

"See, that's what I'm talking about, why he didn't get the nigga money and spend it with you? Why he had to bring a stranger over here on the Drive? He already have them two cats Poochy and Coupe over here."

"If that nigga set me up I'm a kill him and his mother," Dolly says.

"I'm down with you bro. We'll talk later, I got to go. I'll holla," T tells Dolly.

****

Dirty Red goes to Doeboy and says, "Let me get three balls."

Doeboy pulls out a bag full of balls and tells Dirty Red to pick three out. He picks out three then tells Doeboy, "You know Kino the police. Him and Coupe fell out, that's how Coupe got pulled. You ain't notice that when Kino stop coming around hustling, Coupe and Murk was the only one coming back. Poochy went to jail so that's why he stopped coming, but Kino didn't start back coming around until Coupe went to jail. They say he told them crackers about a murder Murk and Coupe did, but he didn't tell on his brother Murk."

"Oh yeah, bet that up bra," Doeboy gives Dirty red some dap and then Dirty Red leaves and starts spreading the lies to all the hustlers on the block. Derick and Pete, the two brothers who kickit with Murk, Kino, Poochy and Coupe. Derick is the one who got caught by the Duke Boys with Poochy, he came to Poochy and told him what he heard about Kino.

"Hell no, that's a lie, Murk and Coupe didn't kill nobody, and Kino didn't set up Coupe to get pulled over. Who spreading them

163

lies?" Poochy asks.

"I don't know, I heard some hoes talking about it."

"Where Murk at?" asks Poochy.

"I don't know, I think him and Pete tricking some jugs at Beretta's house."

All the niggas respect Murk, even the older ones, even though he is only eighteen years old. They know he's crazy as hell, has a don't-give-a-fuck attitude, and is crazy about Kino. So no one says anything about what they heard about Kino around Murk. He's clueless about what' going on. T already doesn't like Kino because Kino told people he sold him some water. It's nothing for T to hear a lie about Kino, not investigate it and run with it. T sees Doeboy and says, "You heard about Kino?"

"I heard he was the police," says Doeboy.

"Dollar told me he thinks he set him up. Kino brought a nigga over to him to buy some work."

"So he set up Dolly?" asks Doeboy.

"That's what Dolly said," T responded.

In a narration recorded by Al- Bukhari, The Messenger of Allah, may peace and blessings be upon him said: *"The angels descend in the clouds and mention matters which has been decreed in heaven; Satan steals a hearing (listens to it stealthily) and communicates it to the soothsayers who tell along with it a hundred lies."*

The truth that Dirty Red told is that Poochy and Kino haven't been on the block since Poochy got jammed by the Duke Boys. And that it wasn't until Coupe got arrested when they started coming back on the block. What the people don't know is why they stop burning the block up and why they started back. T also told some truth which is that Kino brought a stranger to Dolly to buy some work. Just look at how people twist the truth to a lie. Dolly ONLY told T that Kino brought a stranger to him (Bird) to buy some work. But when Doeboy asks T, "So Kino set up Dolly?" T answered, "That's what Dolly said." Dolly never said that Kino set him up. Now Doeboy will tell people, "Kino set up Dolly."

All it takes is some truth, then a person adds a bunch of lies to it and people believe it because of the truth that is being told with it. One lie turns into two, two turns into three, then the story gets twisted, turned and changed from one mouth to another. The sad thing about this is that even if a person doesn't believe in it, they will still spread the lie.

CHAPTER THIRTY-TWO

Its two in the morning and Kino sold out. Becky called two more prostitutes. She had more big money crackers who wanted to get freaked. Kino knows a few people on Polk Street, so he walks over there to find someone who can take him to buy some dope. Niggas gambling and playing Tunk on the trash can on the block. Jugs running up and niggas bum rushing them. It's going on three o'clock in the morning. Kino asks the group of thugs playing Tunk, "Yall seen Bugy?"

"He over there on Dewitt. He went to go re-up."

Kino cuts between the houses to walk towards Dewitt Street and sees Bugy coming from a car parked at Popeye's.

"What's up bra bra?" Kino says.

"Trying to get it bra. What you doing over here this time of night."

"My jug at the Parliament House ran out of dope and I need to re-up."

"The Parliament House, that's a million-dollar motel. All them punks, freaks and lesbians be there. Bra the punks run this city. I never seen or heard of the Duke Boys going over there, but I just left BoBo, he straight, what you trying to get?" Bugy says.

"If he got that iron, I'ma spend two grand. If it's that water, I don't want nothing," Kino says.

"He got that iron bra."

Kino cops four cookies at four fifty a piece. He takes it back to the room and cuts six balls of each cookie. He paid eighteen hundred for the four cookies and cut twenty-four hundred in balls. He thought to himself, "That's a six-hundred-dollar profit in weight. I probably could sell this in balls in one hour in the Palms." He also thought about Bird and Toedoe when Bird told him, "If I have any weight, come sit over there at Big B's with them and I'll sell it all." Kino sat there until Becky and her prostitute went through one of the cookies. He made eleven hundred off that one cookie. It's seven a.m. Kino calls Bugy and asks him if it's straight on Polk Street. He said, "Man, BoBo left to take his kids to school and he ain't coming back 'till tonight. These niggas got to go to Livingston Street or way to South Street to see them Haitians to get right.' "I'm on my way," Kino says.

Kino fronts Becky half a cookie and takes the rest with him to Polk Street to meet Bugy. When Kino gets to Polk Street, he doesn't break nothing down. He sells all balls. Niggas are coming with ninety dollars for a ball and he serves them just to get off the dope. A quick flip is what Kino is thinking and building clientele. He sells all the dope and ends up with thirty-one hundred plus the two hundred he had in his pocket. He then calls Bird to come and get him. Bird comes to get Kino, and they ride back to Pepper tree to take Kino home.

"I just got plugged in bra," says Bird.

"Oh yeah, what you talking about?" Kino asks.

"I got a nigga who sells a half a block for eleven grand. That's fifty-five hundred a quarter. Twenty-seven fifty an eighth. That's like six hundred an ounce. He don't sell nothing under a half. Me and Toedoe are waiting now."

"I don't got no money for no half. I only got thirty-three hundred," Kino says.

"I tell you what. Give me three grand and I'll sell you an eighth out of it, and a hundred and fifty to cook it up," Bird tells Kino.

Bird and Toedoe had exactly eleven grand to buy the half of block. A quarter a piece for the both of them. Bird gave his money to the plug already and he's waiting for the call to come and pick it up. The new plug told Bird not to be coming to his spot in that Chevy on them twenty sixes.
He told Bird to buy him a low key whip or he wasn't going to keep serving him anymore. Kino gave him the money. Bird told him he'll call him when he has it cooked up. Kino said that was good and went to his apartment.
Bird took Kino's three grand and got Mamma Lisa and took her to the car lot to put the car in her name. He put three grand down on a nice clean Toyota Camry for eighty-five hundred.

Murk was walking up when Bird was pulling off. Kino is exhausted from hustling, pulling an all-nighter. Murk is drunk and high as usual. They both are so, so, sooo happy to see their home and bed and be off of the streets. A moment of peace. Home sweet home. They sneaked in quietly trying not to alarm Mrs. B. that they were home. They went to their room, took off their shoes and plopped in the bed with delight. A moment of silence occupies the room as they doze off to sleep within a couple of minutes. It was as if they were in a nightmare, but they were not dreaming. The door busts wide open and Mrs. B. comes in yelling.

"What the hell yall up to? Kino, you ain't been to school and your boss says you quit working at McDonalds. Murk, you smell like smoke and alcohol. You niggas ain't going to be laying up in my house doing nothing with your life. Put your clothes on and get out until you get your head right." She slams the door. Kino and Murk look at each other. Murk has a hangover and Kino has a headache from being woke up quick. They start putting on their sneakers, then all of a sudden, Mrs. B. burst back in the room with a broom in her hand and says, "Yall niggas think I'm playing!"

She rushes Kino and swings the broom at him. "Whop!" The blow landed straight on his back. He gets up and runs out the door. Murk is right behind him and Mrs. B. is right behind Murk. She swings the broom again. "Whop!" right on Murk's back shoulder. Murk senses and reflexes are impaired from the intoxicants, so she has the upper hand on him. He can't move fast enough, "Whop, Whop!" She tears his ass up until he exits the house. She slams the door behind them then staggers back into the living room tired, out of breath, hurt and frustrated. She plops down on the couch and starts crying as she screams, "Lord help me! I can't take it no more. Trying to raise these kids all by myself. Please God, don't let Murk be an addict like his mother! Please Lord, don't let the dope game take Kino to prison like his father."

Kino's Mother is a single, strong, Black woman doing all that she can by herself raising these teenage boys. What I don't understand is how do so many of us Black men, after being incarcerated, don 't come to the realization of what we put our spouses through, the results of our kids growing up in the streets without us, the pain we cause our parents. Then get released from prison and go back to doing the same thing that will land us being incarcerated again. Why? Why? Why? I, Kaleem 'Abdul 'Adl, ask myself the same thing, because I've been to prison before this two hundred and forty-month federal bid. And now I hope that I will have ONE LAST CHANCE to get out and love my soon to be wife the way she supposed to be and deserves to be loved, and be a father to my children. And in shaa'Allah, God willing, be a father to my future children, and take care of my parents who took care of me when I couldn't take care of myself when I was a child, and even now while I'm incarcerated. And most important of all, is to worship my Creator and beg Him the Most High for forgiveness. Prevention is the answer and obedience to the Creator is the best prevention.

CHAPTER THIRTY-THREE

Giovoni comes to bring Dolly ten blocks.

[knocking on the door]

"Who dat?" Dolly says, with his chrome .357 in his hand.

"This Giovoni fool." Dolly lets him in and locks the door behind him.

"Check this out bra. You got to get you a crib in the cracker neighborhood, and that's where we're going to start meeting. I'm a give you a month to get you a spot for us to meet, because I'm not bringing no blocks up in here no more," Giovoni tells Dolly.

"I've been selling dope all my life out these apartments. I done killed niggas over here, robbed niggas, got robbed, got shot, went to prison from these apartments, got out, and here I am. This all I know Giovoni," Dolly tells him.

"You growing Dolly, you ain't coppin' ounces and quarters no more. I'm bringing you ten blocks in this hole. You can't stay the same when you go from ounces to bricks."

"I don't got no job, no credit. The only place I ever lived besides The Palms Apartments is the hotel and prison."

"What about your girl?" asks Giovoni.

"She the same way, all she want to do is smoke weed and fuck all day. I can't even get her to go to school and get her G.E.D. Every time she gets ready to go to school she gets pregnant, then she'll have a miscarriage. She done had five already."

"Probably from all the drugs and alcohol they be using," says Giovoni to himself.

"Look man, I'm going to hook you up with my accountant, he'll get her some check stubs, fix her credit, then she can get a crib, as long as she don't have no record. Turn this spot into your trap house and live in the other spot. You can't keep trapping where you lay your head," Giovani tells him.

"As long as I'm laying with my girlfriend, I'm straight." Then Dolly held up his .357 Magnum.

Giovoni put the duffle bag down on the table and said, "I'll make an appointment with my accountant and let you know. You and your lady just be ready."

"Aight," Dolly says, as Giovoni walks out the door. "Bra!"
"What's up?" Giovoni asks.
"You heard anything about Kino?"
"Nah, like what?" asks Giovoni.
"That he da police."
"Oh yeah! Who said that?"
"T came over here and said he heard that Kino was the police and asked me if I knew anything about it," said Dolly.
"Who told T that Kino was the police?"
"I don't know, I told T that Kino brought some dude over, who said he's from the Bean, over there in Ivey Lane, to buy some dope from me. T said that dude might be the police."
"Alright, I'll see what's up and I'll holla back at cha," Giovoni says.
"G, I tell you, if Kino set me up, I'ma kill him and his mother. And Murk can get it too."
"Hold off until I find out what's up," Giovoni says, then walks out and heads to holla at T.
Giovoni goes to T's house but he ain't home, so G heads to FeeFee's house. He has his own key and goes in.
"What's up boo?" he says, as she runs up and football tackles him, hugs and kisses him.
"You heard anything about Kino?" asks Giovoni.
"I don't know, but Janet said Dirty Red is going around telling everybody that Kino set Dolly up!"
"You talking about that jit who Poochy and Murk was fighting?"

"Yeah. Janet said Dirty Red said he locking down all the jugs and bringing niggas that ain't from the drive over here, and something about Murk and Coupe killed someone. Kino told on Coupe, but didn't tell on his brother Murk, only to get Poochy out of jail," FeeFee says.

"That sounds stupid, because if he tells on Coupe, there's a chance that Coupe will tell on Murk, and that's like telling on both of them. Get your laptop out and see what Coupe is being charged with," Giovoni tells FeeFee.

"What's his name?" FeeFee asks.

"Find out. I'm fin' to go holla at T."
Giovoni leaves to make a couple runs then heads back to The Palms to holla at T.
[knocking on door]
T looks out the window and sees Giovoni at the door, so he opens it.
"What's up G?"
"What's up T? What's this mess about Kino?"
"They say he da police, G."
"And who told you?"
"Dirty Red. And Dolly told me that Kino set him up!" said T. Giovoni smiles and looks at T and says, "Oh yeah?"
"Yeah, they say that nigga who Kino brought to Dolly's house is the feds. The nigga with a blue Chevy sitting on twenty sixes. You know the feds will ride like they're one of us." T doesn't even realize that he's lying on Dolly, and really believes that Dolly told him that Kino set him up.

People who want to believe in a lie or something so bad will start speaking on it over and over to the point where they forget the truth and start believing the lie.

Giovoni is a seasoned veteran and he's been through this situation himself, so he addresses the matter with patience and precaution. He doesn't jump the gun while he carefully analyzes it with wisdom. He knows T is lying because he just spoke to Dolly.

Giovoni figures that T still feels some kind of way about Kino because Kino sprayed his ass about them water cookies T sold Kino. Giovoni also knows that Dirty Red is jealous because Kino is locking down all the power jugs. He's going to try to find out who this person is who Kino brought over to Dolly's house and what Coupe's charges are.

CHAPTER THIRTY-FOUR

Kino and Murk catch a ride to the hotel. They get a room just to get some sleep.

"Nigga, you done got slow. Mama tore your ass up." They both start laughing.

"I thought I was dreaming. I feel like I got to throw up," Murk says.

"Just throw up on your bed and not mines," Kino says. Murk rushes to the bathroom, throws up, and comes back.

"Bro, Bird got a connect, but he only sells a half a block and up," Kino tells Murk.

"For how much?" Murk asks.

"Eleven grand. Between me, you and Poochy, we only need about thirty-seven hundred a piece. If we get a half and Bird and Toedoe get a half, we might be able to get the whole brick even cheaper."

"I probably have around two grand if Mom didn't take it. I left it in the top drawer," says Murk.

"Mom ain't going in the room. We're going to buy her a card and send some roses to her job. I'ma have Tanisha use her mother's credit card and get that done."

Kino is laying on his back on the bed looking at the ceiling talking to Murk. Then all of a sudden he hears the sound of a volcano erupting. He looks at Murk on the other bed and that nigga is gone, snoring his ass off. Kino shakes his head and calls Tanisha.

[Phone ringing]

"Why you didn't call me yesterday?" Tanisha says, answering the phone with a question.

"Whoa Kemosabe," Kino tells her. "Slow your roll boo. Why you ain't call me if you needed me so bad?"

Tanisha is lost for words now. She's trying to play the hard role with Kino and make him sweat her. She wanted to call him so bad yesterday when he didn't call her, but she played her game until he called.

"Cat got your tongue girl?" Kino says.

"I miss you boy. When I'ma see you again?" Kino didn't even care about hearing the answer as to why she didn't call yesterday. He was so happy that she told him that she missed him.

"I'm going to be busy for a couple of days. Then we can hook up. But I need you to do something for me."

"What you need boo?"

"You think you can use your mother's credit card to order my mother some roses and have it sent to her job?

"You know how my mama is, she's going to want double."

"I don't care, tell her I got her." Kino gives Tanisha the information and tells her he'll call her back when he wakes up.

****

Poochy comes home and sees his father's car parked in the yard. He walks into the house and sees his little sister in his father's lap. Mrs. Mabel is cooking, slaving over the stove as usual. He comes in and kisses his mother, speaks to his sister and asks, where's grandpop?"

"At the church," his mother says.

He grills his father and gives his mother a couple of hundred dollars. He goes into his room and counts all the money he's been hustling. Twenty -four hundred dollars. The most money he ever had in his life. His father walks in and sees all the money on the bed.

"Son, I know what you're doing."

"What the fuck do you care about?"

176

[SMACK!] His father slapped him.

"I'm still your father and you're going to respect me."

Poochy balled his fist up and was about to fire back a blow, but something was holding him back.

"Why? Why? Why?" Poochy kept yelling at his father. "Why you beat mama? Why you left us? Why?"

Mr. Mabel started crying and dropped to his knees and said, "I'm sorry son. I'm sorry son. I have a problem. Demons fill my spirit and alcohol brings them out."

"Well stop drinking then!" Poochy yells at his father. Mr. Mabel punches the wall.

"I can't! I can't! I need help son. I need help."

"Don't worry about it. I got it now pop. I'ma get it how I live and you can disappear now."

Mr. Mabel is feeling lower than a piece of dirt on the bottom of a pair of shoes. He cried for help and his son told him to disappear. Mr. Mabel's family doesn't know but he has a new problem added to his alcohol addiction. He puts his head down and walks out of the room then out of the house. La'Quita runs after him screaming.

"Daddy don't go!" Mrs. Mabel is fighting, holding La'Quita from running after him. She and La'Quita are crying while Poochy yells, "Let him go! O coward!"

Poochy's father is six foot four, two hundred and seventy pounds and can woddle. That is fight. In his right mind he would have jacked Poochy up and straightened him, but he's mentally depressed. Once the mind is gone, everything else is downhill. So he gets in his car and leaves.

CHAPTER THIRTY-FIVE

Hard times for a single Black woman raising two young Black men in the ghetto. Her husband has been in prison for close to eighteen years, her son's entire life. She stayed faithful to her husband and struggled to raise their son by herself waiting on D-Bo to come home to her.

"What's wrong Mrs. Betterman?" asks a co-worker who sees the stress in Mrs. Betterman's eyes at work.

"It's so hard raising these boys, keeping them out of the streets, paying rent, going to school, working this job and being alone," says Mrs. Betterman.

"I know girl. My son just went to jail for trying to rob the corner store. I almost caught a heart attack when I got that call from him in jail," says Mrs. B's co-worker.

"I pray to God that Kino don't do nothing like that. And I pray that Murk don't become no addict like his mother."

"Mrs. Betterman, report to the front lobby," was heard coming over the intercom.

"Child, what they want now?" asks Mrs. Betterman.

"I'll walk up with you. I need to use the bathroom anyway," says her co-worker. She really just wants to be nosey and see why they're calling Mrs. Betterman up front.

As soon as they walk into the lobby - "Damn, somebody's in love!" yells her co-worker as she sees two dozen roses and a supersized card.

"I wonder who's that for?" asks Mrs. Betterman.

A man in a tuxedo approaches the two women and says, "Mrs. Betterman?" startling her.

"Yes, that's me," she says.

Her co-worker says to herself, "I knew she wasn't faithful to her husband in prison all these years. Old tricking-ass hoe."

The man in the tuxedo steps forward and says, "A poem for you, Mrs. Betterman," then reads it out loud.

- Mama, you the best, we must confess -
- So please bear me and Murk with patience -
- And we appreciate you for putting up with our mess -
- We're sorry for the stress that we cause -
- We applause, in our eyes you have no flaws -
- And we promise that we're going to move you out of the ghetto -
- So hold us to this. A big house you will move in, so say hello -
- to a new life and to my father you are the best wife -
- So we love you for that, even though you popped us on our back -
- We will always love you no matter what -
- And we mean this with sincerity from the bottom of our hearts -

Your sons,

Tears dropped from her eyes as he handed her the two dozen pink roses, her favorite color, and the card.

CHAPTER THIRTY-SIX

Kino wakes up at 6:00 p.m. at the hotel. He throws a pillow at Murk.

"Wake up! Come on, let's get to the house before mom comes home from work." They call a cab. While waiting, Kino calls Bird.

[phone ringing]

Bird answers, "Yeah?"

"What's up bro?" says Kino.

"Man he talking about tomorrow."

"That's all good bra. I need you to take me to Coupe's mother so I can give her some money to put in his account."

"Man, I need a couple more flips before I can put in my half.

I just bought a low-key to work in, so I got to make up for that."

"What you bought?" asked Kino.

"A clean plain looking Camry with not that many miles on it. I'ma throw a light legal tint on it and ride low key and make it my runner."

"There goes the cab. I got to go. Look like we need a couple of flips ourselves so it's all good. How long will you be before you come take me?" asked Kino.

"I can come now."

"Alright. I'll be home in ten minutes," Kino tells Bird.

"I'll holla."

[click]

Kino calls Poochy when he gets in the taxi cab.

[phone ringing]

"What's up bra?"

"Poochy, you got a hundred and fifty to give Coupe? We all going to put in that amount and Bird is going to take me to Coupe's mother and give her the money."

"Yeah, count me in. When you need it?" asks Poochy.

"Bird on his way now."

"You know I ain't got no car to bring you the money. He coming over here to pick it up?"

"If not Murk got your half, and just give it back to him when you see him," says Kino.

"Look, look. I'll be over there in a couple of hours anyway, so just get it from Murk and I'll see him later tonight. Tell Bird and Mrs. Placky I said what's up."

"Aight."

"I'll holla."

[click]

****

Giovoni sees the Chevy that was described to him, the one that Kino brought to Dolly's apartment. Now it's pulling into Peppertree Apartments where Kino lives. Giovoni rushes over to the car to see who's in it. He sees the driver and Kino getting ready to pull off, so he waves them down before they leave.

"What's up bra bra?" Kino tells Giovoni.

"What's happening bra?" Giovoni says.

"This my boy Bird. He from the Pork-n-Bean. All of us, me, Bird, Murk, Coupe and Poochy went to Ivy Lane Elementary School together, and we just hooked back up," Kino tells Giovoni.

"What's up bra?" Giovoni says to Bird.

"What's happening old G?" Bird responds.

"You know Mama Lisa?" asks Giovoni.

"Yeah, I know her real well," Bird says.

"She still like young niggas I see."

"Naw bra, we ain't like that. We just partners," Bird tells Giovoni.

"You be at Big B's?"

"That's my stomping ground," Bird says.

"I know all them old school niggas from New Malibu and the Old Malibu."

"You talking about T-Rock and them?" Bird says.

"Yeah, him Pooly Cat, Greedy Man, all them old G's," Giovoni says.

"They know me. It's my world now. I'm the new Ivey Lane," Bird says, as he laughs, but he's really dead-ass serious.

"I got much love and respect for them, they are my idols," Bird tells Giovoni.

"Hold on one second," Giovoni says, as he walks away to make a call. He calls Mama Lisa. She was in the tenth grade when Giovoni was in his first year of college and caught her at a party, and had been knocking her off ever since, until he wanted someone more serious.

She was too loose and ghetto to make her his lady, even though she was fine as hell and could stand beside any college girl and knock them out of the box. He didn't find out she was sixteen until she turned seventeen. He had already been sexing her for about a year straight. Mama Lisa had been around with a lot of older men by the time she was eighteen. Her name and image had become ruined. She was a stone cold freak.

Now she's in her thirties with five kids, from five different baby-daddies, stays in the projects, doesn't have a job, and lives off the government. She loves to get high, drink, and gossip about who got what in the city. She can't keep any man her age, but them jitterbugs are on the same level she's on. They're all about getting high and drunk and having sex all day. She can run game on them and pussy whip them jits. Giovoni thanked God that he didn't get her pregnant. He moved on but kept in touch with her because she knew what and with - who and everybody and anything - that was going on in the city. She has all that gossip and she sexes them robbin-ass niggas too. And them robbin-ass niggas know everything. She would be an asset because of the information she obtains.

How often do older men take advantage of younger women and corrupt them instead of loving and guiding them? Win them over with charisma, then dick-whoop them. That's a two-punch combination that knocks the young girl out, leaving her in love, while that man could care less and is on to the next chick. The absence of a father's love in her life plays a role in pushing that young girl to no-good men. A father's love is different from a mother's love. When a father loves his daughter she receives a sense of security, safety, and a masculine type of love that her mother cannot give her. That's why females are attracted to hard rough niggas and not soft niggas. When a female grows up without that masculine love coming from her father, she has a void in her heart. She searches for it from every Tom, Dick and Harry she comes across.

Giovoni corrupted Momma Lisa and broke her heart. A good girl has gone bad. Most women get off the chain searching and trying to keep what they think is love the wrong way.   They don't know what love from a man is because they don't witness it or experience it if their father is not in their lives.

This is why Momma Lisa has five kids with five different baby-daddies. My advice to you men, if you have daughters, be in their lives as much as you can and love them and let them know that they are worth more than a piece of ass. Even my brothers locked up, stay in your daughter's lives, and don't think that just because you're not physically there with her or financially taking care of her, your love for her via cards, letters, phone calls and visits (if you got a good baby-momma) will let her know that her daddy loves her and knowing that alone will go a long way in her heart and mental state when it comes to men.

One last thing – *a stepdad's love is not the same as a biological dad's love; the happiness you can bring to your child's life is unexplainable.*

[phone ringing]

"What's up Giovoni?"
"How you been Momma Lisa?"
"Fine, as long as you ain't trying to sex me."
"Damn girl, you still tripping. That was so long ago. I thought you like young niggas anyway. I'm too old for your ass. Ha! Ha! Ha!"
"Shut up," she says, laughing back.
"Look, I need you to tell me about a jit over that way."
"Who you talking about, G?" asks Momma Lisa.
"His name Bird."
"You talking about Bird who be with Toedoe?"
"I don't know who he be with."
"Do he got a blue Chevy with twenty sixes." Momma Lisa asks

him.

"Yeah, that's him."

"That's my boo, him and Toedoe."

"Damn you fucking both of them?"

"No boy. They look out for me and my kids, and I help them. Them jits getting' money."

"Is he the police, rob or anything like that?" asks Giovoni.

"No, all I know is that they get money and all the old G's respect them."

"Aight, I appreciate ya, hit me up if you need me." She smacks her teeth and says, "Byyy G."

"I'll holla."

[click]

Giovoni walks back to them and tells Kino, "You know they say you the police?"

"What the fuck?" Kino blurted out.

"You was supposed to have set-up Dolly by bringing this person Bird to buy some dope from him," Giovoni says.

"No disrespect bra, but I ain't no fucking police nor is my homie Kino!" Bird tells Giovoni.

"Who said that shit?" Kino asks.

"Look, I'ma handle it, just chill a couple of days 'til the smoke clears," Giovoni says.

Kino tells Giovoni OK out of respect, but his heart tells him to go over to Dolly right now and confront him.

Giovoni left to go handle some emergency business in Brevard County. One of his spots got raided by the police.

Bird took Kino to give the money for Coupe to Mrs. Placky.

****

Murk goes in his top drawer and counts his money. He hustled up to two thousand dollars. This is the most money he ever hustled. This is also the most money he ever had in his life, besides the money he got when he killed the car lot owner, Marlon Carmichael. He's feeling good about himself, so he decided to call Monique, the woman he met at McDonalds. He pulls her business card out and dials the number.

[phone ringing]

"Monique's Salon. How may I help you?"

"Let me holla at Monique," says Murk.

"One moment please," she puts him on hold.

"Monique speaking, how may I help you?"

"What's up boo?" Murk says.

"Who dis?" she says, as she lost her professional voice.

"This Murk, who you met at McDonalds."

"Boy! You tried me. What in the hell happened?"

"I thought the Popos was coming in the front door for me. I had just came from cussing my probation officer out, so I slipped out the side door and hit it. When I realized they wasn't coming after me, I came back to McDonalds, but you were gone."

"Why you just now calling me? I coulda got married by now," she says, laughing.

"I lost your card when I was running and I just now realized your salon was named after you, so I looked it up and that's how I got this number."

"Boy you lucky I like you."

"Nah, you lucky, I like you. So what's up?" Murk says, in a demanding voice which turns her on.

"I got no appointments Thursday, we can hook up then."

"What you want to do, Miss Business Woman?"

"Whatever you like to do, Mr. Thug."

"Can a woman like you tame this thug?"

"Only one way to find out."

"My car is in the paint shop, so you got to come and pick me up," Murk tells her.

"What time?" Monique asks.

"What you like to eat Monique?"

"I love seafood!"

"Aight, come get me at 6:00 p.m. and we'll go to Joe's Crab Shack."

"Sounds like a winner to me" Monique says.

"OK, I'll holla."

"Bye."

[click]

After coming back from taking the money to Mrs. Placky, Bird drops Kino off back at Peppertree. Kino looks at his phone and says, "Who's calling me from this blocked number?"

[phone ringing]

"Hello."

"You have a collect call from Curtis Placky. Press five to accept this call."

"Beeb."

"What's up bra? You should have four hundred and fifty dollars in your account soon. Me, Poochy and Murk put a hundred and fifty dollars together. I just gave it to your mother not too long ago. You remember Bird?"

"From the Pork-n-Bean projects?" Coupe asks.

"Yeah he took me over to your house to give the money to your mother. He said what's up and him and Toedoe giving us a grand toward your bond."

"Damn bro, I appreciate yall. I'm a make it up to ya when I get out, I promise ya."

"You don't owe us nothing but to keep it real," Kino tells him.

"Where Bird and Toedoe at now?"

"Bird left, but I'll see them tomorrow."

"Tell them I said much love and I'll see them when I get out."

"Aight bro, I'll tell them."

"ONE."

"ONE."

CHAPTER THIRTY-SEVEN

Dolly has the ten blocks in his apartment where he lays his head. Giovoni has already told him to find another stash spot. But Dolly doesn't trust anything but his .357, and keeps all the dope and money with him. They say to never smoke a blunt you didn't see rolled up.

Dolly was in the next breezeway smoking with some niggas who just started geeking, that is, crumbling up crack cocaine in a weed blunt. It usually stems from a person boonken, that is, lacing powder in weed. When a person can't get any powder late at night, they can always find someone selling crack. They figure, "I'm not smoking the crack straight up, so I'll just crush the crack rock up and mix it with the weed." The next thing you know; they're smoking crack straight up.

So now Dolly is paranoid, shaking, nervous, flinching from everything that moves, as he walks back to his breezeway. All he's wondering and thinking about is, did Kino set him up? A cop rolls through the breezeway as a regular routine cruise- through. Dolly sees the police car and runs in his breezeway. The officer sees him and parks, then comes after him to investigate why Dolly took off running when he saw him. Dolly tries to get in the apartment, but the door is locked and he dropped his key. He bangs on the door. All he's thinking about are the ten blocks in the apartment and if Kino really did set him up.

His girl is in the shower with the music up loud. She doesn't hear him knocking. Dolly sees the cop coming and says to himself, "I ain't going back to prison," and pulls out that .357 and opens fire on the police. He hits the officer in the chest. He's wearing a vest, but it still knocks him down. Dolly doesn't give him a chance to reach for his weapon. While the officer is falling back, Dolly is running towards him at the same time. By the time the officer hits the ground, Dolly was on top of him, letting loose the rest of the bullets, straight to his head, killing him instantly.

Dolly runs to T's house. The police don't know who the cop- killer is or where he's at. The officer is dead, and they have no witnesses. No one came forward. The Palms Apartments is roped off with police everywhere.

****

Poochy catches a ride over to Kino's house. All three of them are together - Kino, Murk and Poochy.

"Kino, you know they saying you the police," Poochy says.

"Why ain't you tell me, and who you heard it from?" Kino asks. Murk sits up on the bed and says, "Who said that fuck-shit?" "Derick told me he overheard some hoes talking about it," Poochy says.

"Let's go over there now and straighten that shit," Murk says.

"Giovoni told me to chill until he handles everything." Kino says.

"Fuck that. He don't feed us. We getting money on our own," Murk says.

"What Giovoni said?" asks Poochy.

"They talking about that day I brought Bird to Dolly. They think he was the police and I set up Dolly," Kino says.

"I heard you told on Coupe to get me out of jail. Something about Coupe and Murk did a murder and you fell out with Coupe and told on him and not Murk. That's why they pulled Coupe leaving the Palms and you ain't been back since," Poochy says.

"You know we stop selling dope. That's why I ain't been in The Palms, and when I started back I been moving my dope at the Parliament House, Polk Street and having the power jugs meeting me in the back of Pepper tree," says Kino.

"Why your ass didn't tell me?" Murk yelled at Poochy.

"I forgot. I knew it wasn't true, so I didn't pay it no mind," says Poochy.

"Do you know how serious that is? To be called a police-ass nigga? I take that personally," Kino says.

"That's why I brought it up now and told you," Poochy says.

"Man, you was supposed to call me as soon as you heard that shit," Kino told him.

"I know bra. I'm down for whatever, what you want to do?" Poochy says.

"Let's go straighten these niggas," Kino says. Murk gives Kino one gun and he takes the other.

"Damn, I got to get me a gun," says Poochy.

They walk outside and see the whole Palms Apartments is roped off with police everywhere, and the helicopter is overhead. They go back to the house to put up the guns while Bird is calling Kino on the phone.

"What's up bro? What you doing?" asks Bird.

"Fin to go straighten that mess."

"Didn't Giovoni tell you to chill until he handles it? I done found out who Giovoni is. That's who we really need to holla at bro. But they say he tells everybody he through and don't do nothing."

"I don't see him doing nothing over here either," says Kino. "What's up? Yall want to ride with me and Toedoe to Tampa? They say Club Atlanta poppin' tonight."

Kino takes the phone from his ear and asks them if they want to ride with Bird and Toedoe to Tampa.

"I thought we was going to handle that police shit," Murk says. "There's a time and place for everything. Hot as it is

over there,
now is not the right time. My father used to tell me that all the time," Kino says.

"Yeah, let's ride!" Poochy says.

Kino tells Bird to come and get them.

"I'm on my way."

[click]

****

Dolly is hiding in T's house; the police never saw where Dolly ran to because he was dead. Dolly walks in T's house.

"What in the hell happened?" T asks Dolly. He's geeked up, high and paranoid, and not thinking rationally.

"The police were coming after me from when Kino set me up.
I ain't going back to prison bra, so I killed that cracker."

"Oh yeah! I knew that nigga was no good."

"I'ma kill that nigga!" Dolly says.

"What's up, whenever you ready bro!" T says.

"As soon as it cool down. Get me some yayo."

T calls this chick named Shelia to bring out the silver plate. A silver colored plate. T gets a couple of quarter keys he bagged up and took all the shake from both bags. It added up to a little over an ounce. He dumped it on the plate, then he, Dolly and the chick had a snorting party. They plotted and planned how they were going to kill Kino. And if Murk got in the way, they would kill him too. The chick just laughed at everything they said, except when Dolly said one thing.

"If that nigga ain't home when we go over there, I'ma wrap his mother up and make her fuck my girlfriend. Then he held his .357 up and they started laughing.

The chick, who was snorting with them, wasn't laughing because she'd been in that situation before when some slimy-ass niggas made her suck all their dicks, then ran a train on her when she was only fifteen years old, living with her big time Uncle who they tied up and killed.

They continued to snort, plot and plan until the police activity slowed down.

CHAPTER THIRTY-EIGHT

Bird's 1980 box Chevy is floating like a boat heading West down I-4. Music is blasting and heads are banging to Slick Vick, Look Cool Jock, Jam Pony Express CD on their way to Club Atlanta in Tampa, Florida, a city that's about an hour's drive give or take, from Orlando. Tampa's clubs are thugged-out like the O and they're off the chain too. They also support their local artists. They have their own sound. Some call it jook music. They are also down with the dirty south vibe, especially Florida music.

"Fire up the blunt," Murk tells Toedoe.

Kino doesn't smoke and doesn't like to be smoked out in the car, and he's usually the only one thinking.

"What yall going to do when them crackers pull us over in Tampa? We out of town niggas, car on twenty sixes, late at night, and as soon as the cracker walk up to the car to ask for your license and registration, and smell the weed, he's going to call the dogs, make them bark, then search the car and get all these pistols we got in here. Now we locked up in jail out of town."

"Nigga, you just saying that because you don't smoke," Murk says, as he fires up the blunt.

"Nigga, don't hog up the weed. Puff and pass, not puff and hold," Toedoe says. Kino shakes his head and cracks his window.

They arrive in Tampa and exit off Howard and Armenia.

They cross over Armenia and turn on Howard. They ride down to Kennedy and make a left, then ride to the club on the left-hand side.

"He bustin' your ass Bird," says Poochy, as a candy apple red box Chevy with cherries painted in the paint, gutted out in crush solid cherry red color, sitting on Amani twenty-eight platinum Vorando's blasting Rick Ross, "Every Day I'm Hustling" out of twelve Kicker twelves powered by Fosgate amps, shaking Bird's car.

"What in the hell he got in there?" asks Poochy, as they ride by them.

Some other niggas riding behind that box Chevy are hanging out all the windows, shaking their dreads, yelling "West Tampa nigga," looking at Bird and them crazy.

"Damn, look at all that ass," Toedoe screams.

"Man, there some hoes down here in Tampa," Kino says.

" I'm a get me a black donk with black guts on thirties and crush all yall niggas," Murk says.

Murk hangs out of the car and yells at some chicks walking to the club, "O-town baby."

One of them yells back, "Jackson Height nigga."

"Stop the car, stop the car!" Murk yells to Bird, who stops.

"What's up boo? What's your name?"

"Shanice."

"You and your friends meet us at the bar and I'll holla at you then," Murk told her.

"Nigga, you can't afford this riding in the back seat O broke-ass nigga."

"O nappy head bitch! I'll buy your ass if I want to," Murk yells back.

"Nigga, my hairdo cost more than your whole outfit."

"Bitch, you probably bald headed. Give that horse back his hair," Murk says, and all the girls start laughing.

"There goes the police yall, chill," Kino says to Murk.

They park and go into the club, and the DJ Rocking Rod is screaming out the hoods.

"One time for College Hill, them niggas for real; one time

for Review Terrace, them niggas kill; Royal Park, don't go there after dark; Barna Height, making them crackers leave in flight; one time for West Tampa Projects, Ponce DeLeon, them boys getting money at the Honky Tonk. As he called out the hoods, you could see the niggas and chicks get rowdy as they represent their block.

"Let's get a bottle," Toedoe says.

They find an area and chill and tell a waiter "Two bottles of Grey Goose." The chick who Murk was arguing with walks up to him and grabs his ass.

"Damn Miss Sassy Mouth, all that shit you was talking. Why you jocking me now?" says Murk.

"Boy, you know you want this," she says, as she turns around and bounces her ass, making it jiggle. "You going to buy me and my girls a drink?"

Those of you who are reading this book already know how this story will go. Murk brought all of his money that he hustled up with him.

"As a matter of fact boo!" Murk pulls out a knot of money, flossin' with his whole life's savings. "A bottle for you and for your girls."

Bird, Poochy, Toedoe and Kino are talking to each other.

"Who taking the fat girl?"

"Who taking the ugly one?",

"She ugly, but she fine as hell and look like she can suck the brains out of you. I want her," Toedoe says.

"Shoot, fat girls got the best pussy," Poochy says.

Kino takes off walking towards the best looking one left before Bird tries to get her. Bird shakes his head and yells, "Kino you think your ass slick," while Kino goes to holla at the baddest chick left.

****

Meanwhile, back at The Palms Apartments, T and Dolly fucked the shit out of the chick, then T sends her ass home and tells her to get out, "we got some business to handle."

Sheila is drunk and high and has nowhere to go.

"You know I got nowhere to go T," Sheila pleads with him.

"I don't care bitch, we got to handle that nigga Kino."

He pushed her out the front door after he and Dolly both got their nut. She walks over to FeeFee's house and she lets her in.

"Girl, why your clothes half way put on and falling off your body?" FeeFee asks her.

"T just rushed and kicked me out of his house. He wouldn't even let me put my clothes all the way back on."

"What in the hell is he up too? Why he tripping? Don't he know someone killed a police officer in front of Dolly's apartment. It's hot as hell around here while they looking for the cop killer." FeeFee looks at her and says, "Why you got quiet all of a sudden?"

"I just don't feel too good," she tells FeeFee.

"Aight, go on in the room.   I just changed the sheets in the guest room."

"Thank you FeeFee."

"You got to be smarter girl, and stop letting these niggas use you then throw you to the side like a piece of rag."

"My daddy didn't love me, so who else will if my own father don't love me?"

This is the result of a father not being in his daughter's life. Daddy's little girl is all she ever wanted to be. Her uncle loved her, but it wasn't enough, and when he got killed, Sheila had nobody else. So now she's looking for love in all the wrong places, and from all the wrong men.

****

Dolly walks to his apartment and sees it roped off and a couple of police still there, so he calls his girl.
-phone ringing-

"Boy, where in the hell you been!? I been calling your

phone! These crackers scaring me. Someone killed the police outside our door."

"What they say to you?" asks Dolly.

"I told them I don't know who did it. I was in the shower when I heard the gunshots. I went on about my business and shortly after they came knocking on the door. They left after I told them shots are fired all the time around here so it's normal to me. I'm scared Dolly. When you coming home bae?"

"Tomorrow, when they leave. Just hold tight and stay in the house, and don't answer the door for no one. Did they ask about me or try to search the house?"

"No, they just wanted to know if I seen or heard anything. I told them all I heard was some gunshots while I was in the shower."

"Aight, just hold tight boo, and I'll see you tomorrow."

"You promise Dolly?" cries Renae.

"Yeah girl, stop whining! I said I'll be there!" demanded Dolly. He hung up the phone and walked back to T's house.

- knocking on T's door –

"Who is it?" T said.

"It's me Dolly, fool." T opens the door and lets him in.

"What it look like at your house?"

"Police still there, but not like it was earlier. I talked to Renae on the phone and she good. They didn't try to go in the house. Giovoni just dropped off ten blocks."

"Them crackers think they're slick. They trying to act like they not looking for ya, so they can catch you slipping. That police was coming for you, don't forget that. That's why you had to kill him and this is all Kino's fault."

"I don't know bro; it's not adding up. Why they didn't go in the house?" Dolly asks.

"You know how they do when you're under investigation? They let you go. Don't fuck with you, and wait - so they can catch you with everything. Take another bump bro and get your mind right so we can go do this nigga!" T yells all skeeted up.

T hands Dolly some more coke and they both start back snorting.

****

At Club Atlanta, Kino and his click are drunk as a skunk. The chicks they met are drunk as well. The females went to the bathroom.

"I told her straight up a hundred dollars," Bird says. "What she say?" asks Poochy.

"Nigga, what you think? She said yeah."

"Hell no, that fat bitch told me two hundred, and three if I want head included," Poochy says.

They all start laughing.

"I done gave that bitch a hundred already," Murk says.

"What's up with you Kino?" asks Bird. "Since you ran so fast to lock the sexy one down."

"Man, she talking about she got a boyfriend and she just wanted to get out of the house and go clubbing with her long lost friends and sister."

The music stops as silence fills the air for two seconds. Then all of a sudden a computer voice blasts out of the speakers. "Four hundred de-gree-ee-ss," then the beat and Juvenile's voice plays at the same time. "*You see me, I eat, sleep, shit and talk rap. I seen that '98 Mercedes on T.V. I bought that. I had some felony charges, I fought that ...*" The crowd went crazy. All of them girls started backing it up on Murk and his crew except the one who Kino was with. She went to dancing but not all on Kino.

The big girl was poppin' that ass, bent over with her hands on her knees, grinding on Poochy. Poochy grabs her hips from behind and starts doing the California Worm and poppin'. Everybody starts laughing. Then Toedoe yells, "Work Poochy! Work Poochy!" Kino says, "Oh no! Why you want to tell him that?" Then the girls start laughing and start yelling along with Toedoe, "Work Poochy! Work Poochy!

Work Poochy!" Poochy did the electric slide and ended up in front of the big girl and started poppin'. Then all of a sudden the women started yelling, "Go Cheryl! Go Cheryl! Go Cheryl!"

Crazy as this sounds, she started poppin' and shaking her big ass making everything vibrate, then she stopped and acted like she grabbed Poochy's head, placed it on the ground, then jumped up in the air and landed in a split on top of where his head is supposed to be. The crowd burst out laughing and everybody said, "Damn!" when she landed. Her friends started high-fiving and falling on each other laughing.

Bird and Kino were laughing so hard they almost fell. Poochy couldn't do anything but laugh at his defeat, but he told Toedoe, "Boy, she flexible. I'm a spread them legs like a pretzel and bang that fat pussy while yall laughing."

After a few more songs play, they leave the club and go to Gyro's Subs and order some food. They all head to their cars and Bird follows them to Busch Boulevard to get some rooms.

They pull into the Red Roof Inn. Bird and Toedoe get one room and they tag team them hoes. Poochy and Murk get a room and knock their boots. Kino takes Bird's car and takes Reatha home in Jackson Height.

"What bar is that?" Kino asks.

"The Honkey Tonk Bar," Reatha says.

"This remind me of Dixie Doodle on Paramore in Orlando," Kino says. Niggas are everywhere, basers trying to buy dope, hoes turning tricks. "It's off the chain over here," Kino says.

She won't give Kino her number, but she takes his, then he drops her off and heads back to Busch Boulevard. He thinks about everything that's going on. How his life is moving so fast and he's wondering if he's on the right course.

The first thing he thinks about is his father, D-Bo. How he grew up his whole life without him. He's also thinking about why he quit his job, stopped going to school, Poochy's charges, Coupe being locked up and his mother being mad and disappointed at him. He still hasn't talked to her since she ran him and Murk out of the house with her broom. He thought about Tanisha, and how he wants to really love her. Then it hit him. He got a sick feeling in his stomach all of a sudden, as soon as he thought about Dolly and people saying he's the police.

He doesn't know why he's feeling the way he's feeling. What he does know is that something's not right. He goes up to the room and the chicks left. They are all in one room talking about who's pussy is the biggest. They stay up talking about back in the days when they were in Ivey Lane Elementary school until they all fell asleep in the one room. There's no driving back to Orlando tonight. They're drunk, tired and fucked out, except Kino. He's stressed out thinking about the consequences of what's happening in his life.

******

Back in Orlando, T and Dolly dress up in all Black, load their pistols up, and walk across the street to Peppertree.

"Call down to the party house and see if Murk is there," Dolly says.

"Aight," replied T.

-phone ringing –

"What's up T?"

"What's up Moley?"

"Aay, Murk down there with yall, I need him to do something for me?"

"Nah bra, I ain't seen him all night."

"Aight, bro, I'll holla." [click]

"He ain't there," T told Dolly.

"That means he probably home with Kino. This is what we going to do. Knock on his window and tell him the police are chasing us, and we need to hide in his house. When he comes to the door to let us in, that's when we'll wrap him up," says Dolly.

They knock on the window and nobody responded. "They must not be in there," T says.

"Fuck that, his mother is. I ain't playing with this police-ass nigga. I'ma let him know he better not come to court or else his mother will pay," Dolly says.

"How are we going to get her?" asks T.

"We're going to knock on the door and tell her Kino is down the street and got shot. When she opens the door to let us in, we got her. You got to be panicking, scared and concerned so she'll open the door," says Dolly.

[Knock! Knock!]
[Knock! Knock!] [Knock! Knock!]

"Now who that is knocking on my door this time of night?" Mrs. B. says to herself. The first thing that comes to her mind is her son and Murk. Hoping nothing happened to them, she puts on her robe and bedroom slippers then comes to the door while they're still knocking.

"Who is it knocking on my door this time of night?" Mrs. B. asks.

"Mrs. Betterman! It's Kino, he's been shot across the street."

The next thing that came to Mrs. B's mind was guilt for kicking him out. Now she feels like it's her fault and Kino is her only son. She rushes quickly to open the door and hear what's going on. To her surprise, when she opens the door, Dolly rushes her, slapping her with the pistol, sending her to the ground. She screams and he slaps her again and tells her, "Shut up bitch. The more you scream the more I'ma whoop your ass."

T comes in and closes the door behind him.

Mrs. B. flashes back to the time when she got home-invaded and raped because of her husband's dealings in the streets. She starts shaking convulsively as she cries, stuttering with slob and blood coming out of her mouth.

"I have no money, take whatever you want. Please just don't hurt me or violate my body."

"Shut up and listen. One thing I hate is a police-snitching-ass nigga and the only thing I hate more than that is the police- ass nigga that set me up. And your son Kino. That's what he did. Set me up."

"What are you doing? Please don't rape me!"

He looks into her eyes and takes the gun and caresses her face, stroking up and down as if he's trying to wipe the blood off her face with the barrel of the gun.

"Suck the blood off this gun. I want to see you swallow this barrel."

Shaking and crying, Mrs. B. relapsed from this repeated incident. All she could think about is that this is happening all over again over drugs that she didn't sell or use.

"Swallow it, all the way down to the trigger bitch," Dolly says. Her face is swollen and bleeding from Dolly pistol-whipping her. He's been smoking crack and weed, snorting cocaine and drinking alcohol all night. His sympathy level is zero. Mrs. B. is innocent and now a victim from her son's involvement with drugs.

> We as drug dealers hardly ever think about the evil things that happen from being involved with an unhealthy environment. What's so strange is that the one who does something wrong hardly ever recompense the evil consequences of their behavior in this life. Or at least that's what it seems like. The innocent ones around the evil person reap the repercussions of the evil one's actions. I've seen too many times where the peon gets all the time of incarceration, while the kingpin or the person going

around killing people robbing people, shooting people, gets less time or a slap on the wrist. Or that cousin, brother, or friend that's not in the streets and rides with his bad ass cousin, etc., who is always doing something evil to someone but never gets hurt, shot, or in trouble. Instead, it's just the good cousin who just took a ride with him who ends up getting shot. Would it be fair to assume that if Kino and Murk were never selling dope, Dolly wouldn't be there pistol-whipping and sexually abusing their mother?

"I'm not going to fuck you, but my girlfriend will." Mrs. B. almost had a heart attack when Dolly's girlfriend got through sexing her.

Then Dolly told Mrs. B., "Tell Kino, don't go to court and you'll be safe."

Dolly and T leave then they run back across the street to T's house.

****

The hotel maids are knocking on the door asking them are they going to stay another night or check out.

"What time is it?" Bird asks.

"Eleven o'clock," Kino says.

"We checking out!" Bird yells to the maid through the door, as he looks at his phone. Then he says, "Oh man, that's the connect. I missed his call."

"Call him back!" Kino and Toedoe say simultaneously. They get up and get themselves together and head back to Orlando.

"Somebody called me from a blocked number and left a message," Kino says. He checks the message -

"This is Agent Byron McMills, and I'm at the hospital with your mother. She has been home-invaded and the suspects were mentioning your name. So please call me at 407-555-5555 so I can interview you to help me catch these maniacs."

Kino yells out, "F-U-C-K! S-H-I-T! Damn it man! I'ma kill those motherfuckers! "

"What! What! What Kino?" everybody asks.

"It's mom, Murk!"

"Mom, what about mom!" Murk yells back.

"Someone home-invaded her and she's in the hospital. He said they were mentioning my name."

"Who said that?" asked Bird.

"Some agent who wants to ask me some questions."

Kino starts calling his mother's phone and gets no answer.

He calls Orlando Regional Medical Center to see if she's a patient there.

"Take me to the hospital Bird, she's there."

It's a long ride back to Orlando. Silence fills the air as tears fall from Kino and Murk's eyes.

Poochy starts thinking about his father and tears up too. Bird and Toedoe feel bad. They are ready and down for whatever. They try to break the ice on this long ride home by cracking on Poochy.

"Damn Poochy, I believe Big Girl got you pussy-whipped. I ain't never heard a nigga make more noise than the girl when he nuts.

"She ain't got me pussy whipped," says Poochy.

"There is one thing I know she whipped."

"What's that?" asks Poochy.

"She whipped your ass on that dance floor last night!" They all bust out laughing except Murk and Kino. Kino shows a fake smile, but not Murk, he got straight killing on his mind.

They make it to the hospital and go straight to her room. Kino and Murk bust in the room and runs to her. Kino hugs her like a little boy who was lost at an amusement park and then found his parents. He starts crying saying, "Mom, I'm sorry! Who was they?"

Murk is in the corner crying. He can't even look at her.

Poochy, Toedoe, and Bird stand at the entrance of the door and give them their time.

Finally, Kino lets go of her and Mrs. B. looks at Murk balled up on the floor in the corner and says "Murk, come here baby," and holds her arms out towards him. He yells out, spitting snot out of his nose as saliva cakes up on the side of his mouth saying, 'Mama! Mama! I love you mama! " as he runs and hugs her. All three of them are crying. A scene so devastating, even the nurse walks away with tears falling.

Poochy, Toedoe, and Bird walk over there with tears falling down their faces too and greet her.

One of her eyes is Black and swollen. Part of her head is shaved, because the doctor had to put staples in it to close the wound. Her stress level was near heart attack stage. Her blood pressure was so high they're going to keep her until it returns to normal.

"Hello Poochy," Mrs. B. says.
"Hello Mrs. B. I'm sorry for what happened to you."
"Is that Bird and Toedoe?" Mrs. B. asks.
"Yes ma'am. We sorry too," they say as they kiss and hug her.
"Yall still look the same. Are yall boys staying out of trouble?"
"Yes ma'am," they answered.
"Mom, tell me what happened," Kino said.

Mrs. B told everything from the knock on the door until the police came. When she started telling them the sex acts they made her perform, Murk stormed out of the room, slammed the door, and flipped the chairs over in the waiting room. He started thinking about his twin sister being molested by his biological mother's husband. That's when Murk went to the corner of the room, dropped to the floor, balled up like a little baby, and started crying again.

After hearing the home invaders were abusing his mother because they thought that he set them up, Kino really broke down because of the guilt he felt, even though he didn't set nobody up. He never felt guilty in his life. Bird even felt guilty as veins started popping in his head hearing what happened and looking at Mrs. B's staples in her head, and her Black eye.

All of them kissed and hugged Mrs. B. then told her that they loved her. They apologized for what happened then headed back to the house.

CHAPTER THIRTY-NINE

Kino and his click are at the apartment in Peppertree. They walk in and see blood in the living room. This only flares up their emotion as all of them walk in and sit down and contemplate about what they're going to do.

Poochy, Bird and Toedoe are cleaning the blood up and putting the furniture back in place, while Murk heads straight to his room and Kino sits down. Kino's phone rings, and he answers it.

"You have a collect call from Curtis Placky ..."
"Yeah," Kino says, answering in a despairing voice.
"What's wrong with you? What's going on?" Coupe asks with concern. Kino tells him all the details.

When Coupe hangs up the phone, he goes back to his cell with his head down, pouting like a big baby about to cry. One of the older, stupid, playing-ass niggas who takes everything as a joke, is a forty-year-old man named Danny Boy, who's still kiki and plays all day every day, because he has no life of his own. He never knows when it's time to be serious and stop playing. But he's not so stupid that he doesn't know who not to play with. He looks at Coupe as a scary little jit who's not going to do anything.

"What's wrong jit? You found out that your tricking-ass hoe fucking?" Danny Boy says, as he laughs out loud, along with a few of his followers.

Coupe cuts his eyes at him with a unit that could kill, but he doesn't say anything. Danny Boy took that silence from Coupe as a yes. Being hyped up by a few of his followers, he ignores Coupe's killer look, and takes him as a joke. Danny Boy knows he'll whip Coupe's ass if he thinks about trying him.

"What's wrong jit? Jodei got your girl bent over knocking her brains out? Ha! Ha! Ha!" Danny Boy says, while everybody starts laughing.

"Nah. Jodei got your mother turning tricks," Coupe said. All of his followers burst out laughing harder at Danny Boy than they were laughing at Coupe.

"Boy, I'll whip your ass talking that shit!" Danny Boy said. He's not laughing anymore as he walks towards Coupe. This teenager's emotions flared up because he's scared. He's also frustrated and hurt by the treatment of his father, and he's mad. Coupe is experiencing an environment that he's not immune to for the first time in his life. He doesn't know anyone in the cell with him, and there's no officer around to help him if Danny Boy and his click jump him. Danny Boy is all up in Coupe's face, pointing his finger at him, about to poke his eye out.

"What you say about my mama, fuck-boy?" Silence fills the room as Boogy, Big Ant and Mouse come out of their cell.

"Slap that nigga, Coupe!" Big Ant yells out. "Them niggas ain't going to do nothing," he says.

"Let them fight," the Old G Boogy tells Big Ant. Then he yells to everyone else standing around - "Ain't nobody going to jump in." He turns to Big Ant and says, "Let Coupe become a man. This is his test to become strong and survive in the gutter or be weak and become a pushover."

Coupe is a seventeen-year-old boy who's never been to jail. He was raised as a middle-class child who always had more than the lower class kids he grew up with. He does not know the definition of struggle or fighting for himself. When he fought in the club helping Kino, he threw chairs from a distance. When he fought in the Palms Apartments helping Poochy and Murk, he had a stick and was hitting them niggas from behind, while they were fighting his homies. Now he has a grown man who is twice his age and twice his size all in his face, smashing his fingers in his forehead calling him a fuck-boy in front of everybody "

Coupe looks around for something to grab, but everything is bolted down. He sees no weapon to use. He has to rely on his own hands for the first time in his life. That last poke to his forehead was the last straw. Coupe swings with all his might on Danny Boy, and connects.

Danny Boy said, "That's all you got?" and swings back on Coupe, knocking him on his ass. Coupe gets up and runs to the nearest room and grabs the plastic top to the gray box that they give everybody to keep their belongings in. Coupe runs back out of the room and charges Danny Boy, swinging the top and crying at the same time. He connects and splits Danny Boy's face open above the eye. That was all Coupe needed to see was blood, and he let loose like a pitbull tasting blood in a dog fight.

He went to swinging that top, left and right. Danny Boy is now in defensive mode, back peddling. Coupe connects again in the same spot, busting the cut open wider as more blood runs out. The officers rush in and tackle Coupe, smashing his head on the concrete, rough him up a bit, then cuff him. They take him and Danny Boy straight to the hole.

CHAPTER FORTY

"Ballistics Department. How may I help you?"

"This is Agent Byron McMill. Is lab analyst Baker available?"

"Hold please," the receptionist tells him.

"Mr. Baker, Agent Byron McMill is on line one."

"Thank you." Mr. Baker pushes line one. "Yes, how may I help you Agent McMill?

"Were you able to get the ballistics on case number 147?"

"Yes, the 9mm shells recovered in the killings of the ex-police dogs are the same kind of shells found at Marlon Carmichael's car lot. Different 9mm guns were used, but they're the same bullet casings."

"So basically the bullets came from the same box of ammo?" asks the agent.

"Perhaps. They're the same brand, the same kind."

"So it's possible that the same person used bullets with the same casings, but fired them from two different guns?"

"Yes, that could be true. Also, the bullets you pulled out of Marlon Carmichael and sent us do not match any of the guns we tested," said analyst Baker.

"So the guns used in these killings are still out there in the streets?" asks Agent Byron.

"Yes," replied the lab tech.

"What about the bullet that was found in the back seat of Curtis Placky's car?"

"That bullet matches the owner's gun, not the one involved in the murder. "

"That means the owner of the dogs is telling the truth," Agent Byron said to himself.

"OK, I will try to get these guns to see if we can get a match,"

Bryon told the tech.

"You get the guns, you got the murderer," says the lab tech.

"Thank you sir. You be good until further notice," Agent Byron told him.

"OK sir." - click -

Agent Byron calls his informant.

- phone ringing -

"Yeah! who dis calling me blocked?"

"This is your life saver, asshole!" replied Agent Byron.

"Sir, sooo sorry. How can I assist you?"

"What you know about Curtis Placky?"

"Oh, you talking about Coupe?" "That's what people call him?"

"Yeah, he hangs with a dude name Kino. I heard that's who got him over there in the Palms."

"Tell me about Kino," demands Agent Byron.

"He sells dope and has a brother name Murk."

"Do you know anything about any murders from these people?" asks the agent.

"No, not that I know of, but Kino sells a lot of dope, I do know that."

"Is this the Kino who lives at Peppertree?"

"Yes."

"His mother just got home-invaded, and the attackers were calling his name."

"I didn't know that," the informant says.

"It just happened last night. Keep me posted on these guys if you want to stay free," says Agent Byron.

"Yes sir, I'll see what I can do."

"You better, or else!" Then the agent hangs up in the informant's face.

CHAPTER FORTY-ONE

Angela Bernard is Mrs. Betterman's sister. She's also Murk's mother's best friend, and she came to see D- Bo.

D-Bo is walking the track with his Christian brother and his Muslim celly. The Christian brother calls D- Bo's celly.

"Abdush-Shukar?"

"What's up?" he replies.

"Why do you Muslims say that the White men are devils and the Black men are gods?"

"Subhana Allah! That is not the belief of a Muslim and a degradation to God-Almighty who is far above what they ascribe to him. We believe that He the Most High is the only ONE worthy of being worshiped in truth. We also believe that all mankind is created from Adam. His wife Eve was created from Adam's rib. All of the human race is created from them two. In other words, we all came from Adam," says Abdush-Shukar.

"The White people too?" asks D- Bo.

"Yes. Allah, who you call God-Almighty, created Adam with His Own Hands, from the earth. The Prophet Muhammad, peace and blessings be upon him, speaks about all of the different colors of dirt, like White sand, red clay, Black dirt, and so on used to create different peoples. This explains why there are different colors of people that all came out of Adam' s lineage."

"So why do Muslims say that the White men are devils and other Muslims say that they are gods?" asks the Christian brother.

"These are not the teachings or the belief of Muhammad Ibn 'Abdullah, peace and blessings be upon him, who was the last and final messenger and prophet sent to all mankind and Jinns before the Last Day." He continues. "The Nation of Islam follows Elijah Muhammad and call themselves Muslims. The Moorish Science Temple follows Drew Ali, and call themselves Moorish Muslims. And The Five Percenters, who claim they are God, follow Clarence 13th X, and call themselves Muslims too, and many more besides these. But if you don't follow Prophet Muhammad, peace and blessings be upon him, and believe everything he came with, then you are not a Muslim, but just making a claim to be one. You can't say you believe in Prophet Muhammad, peace and blessings be upon him, while at the same time follow someone else who opposes what Allah and Muhammad say, and claim you're a Muslim," says 'Abdush-Shukar.

"It does sound crazy to say that you're a God. But one thing I do know is that Jesus is God," says the Christian brother.

"If Jesus is God, then who is Jesus praying to when he falls on his face and prays? Does God have a God?" asks D-Bo.

The Christian brother pauses to gather his thoughts to answer D-Bo's question.

During that pause, 'Abdush-Shukar says, "Laysa kamith lihee shayoon."

"What you said?" both D-Bo and his Christian brother ask simultaneously.

"Allah Ta'Ala says in the Quran, verse 42:11, translated to mean, "*There's nothing like unto Him.*" This means He the Most High is nothing like His creation, and all human beings were created and exist by Allah's will, including Jesus, who we call 'Easa, son of Maryam, peace be upon him."

"Jesus wasn't created!" yells D-Bo's Christian brother.

"Allah says in the Quran that Jesus, son of Mary, peace be upon him, is a word from Allah, and that word was BE! Allah said BE!, and Jesus, son of Mary, peace be upon him, was then created into existence as a human being, in the womb of Mary. This is why he ate and slept like a human being and was limited to whatever a human being is limited to. Unlike God-Almighty, who doesn't eat nor sleep, or have a limit to what He, the Most High, can do," says 'Abdush-Shukar.

"I never thought of it like that," says D-Bo.

"All I know is that my mother, my grandmother, and my family believes in Jesus and He is God," says the Christian brother.

"We believe in Jesus, peace be upon him, too. We love him,

respect him and honor him as one of the greatest Messengers sent by Allah to the Children of Israel," says 'Abdush-Shukar.

"I thought yall Muslims didn't believe in Jesus," says D-Bo.

"If we don't believe in Jesus, peace be upon him, then we are disbelievers, and are going to the hellfire for eternity. We just don't believe he's God, therefore we don't worship him.

There's only ONE God and He's the only ONE worthy of being worshiped," says 'Abdush-Shakar.

"Derick Betterman, report to visitation," comes over the prison-wide intercom system.

"I wonder who that could be?" said D-Bo.

"You know Little Mamma still loves you," his Christian brother says, punching him playfully.

"I'll holla at yall man, and we got to finish this conversation."

"You have a good one," 'Abdush-Shakar tells him.

D-Bo gets dressed and walks through the doors to see Angela Bernard, his sister-in-law. They hug and greet each other then sit and talk.

She tells D-Bo about Mrs. B getting home-invaded and sexually assaulted. She lets him know that Kino is in the streets. Then she tells him about Murk, something D-Bo had an inclination to, but he ignored it, and now he knows it's true.

After the visit was over, D-Bo went right back to his dorm and immediately called his wife.

CHAPTER FORTY-TWO

After Kino had hung up the phone with Coupe, he sat on the couch in the living room. Toedoe and Bird finished cleaning up the blood and asked Kino where to put the dirty rags. Bird puts up the chemicals in the cabinet then they all sit down on the couch.

"T-Rock from old Malibu has a chopper for sale," Bird says.
"How much he want for it?" asks Kino.
"I don't know, but I'll find out," he replied.
"This fuck-nigga really think we set him up," Kino tells Bird.
"It's got to be more to it than that," Toedoe says.
"You got Giovoni's number?" asked Bird.
"No, I'ma handle this! Waiting on him is what got my mother in the hospital now. I need some fire with a silencer," says Kino.
"I think Derick and Pete know someone who can get us any kind of guns," says Poochy.
"Aight, look. Poochy, you go get Derick or Pete and tell him to hook us up with that connect on the guns. Bird, find out how much T-Rock wants for that chopper. We going to flip this bomb of dope, buy the guns, then kill this nigga," says Kino.
"I'ma get Murk to walk over there with me," says Poochy.
"I'ma check that out now." Poochy calls Murk.
"Aye Murk." They all look to the room, waiting for Murk to emerge as Poochy calls him again. "Murk!" Poochy calls him again, but gets no response. Everybody gets a funny feeling and realizes that he's not there elaborating with them about what they're going to do. They all rush to the bedroom to see if he's alright. They open the door and to their surprise, he's not there, and the window's open.

"Shit," yells Kino. They already know where he went and what he went to do.

****

Murk already knows how Dolly answers the door with his .357 in hand. He told himself he's not going to give Dolly a chance to shoot him. Murk has to be crazy, because it's in the middle of the day, bright daylight, and everybody's out.

He approaches Dolly's breezeway. The neighbor upstairs looks at Murk and Murk looks at him as he goes back into his apartment. Murk knocks on Dolly's door, then places both his hands in his hoody sweatshirt's pockets as he grips both of his Glock 9's.

Renae is still waiting on Dolly to come back. She was about to answer the door, then she remembered Dolly telling her not to answer it for anyone. She stays still, trying not to make any noise. Murk starts banging on the door and the neighbor from upstairs comes back out of his apartment, looks at Murk and says, "Dolly ain't there, he ain't been there since yesterday. I'm waiting on him too."

Murk looks up at him, then a familiar voice calls Murk's name from a distance. "Murk!" It's Kino and them. Kino walks up to Murk and grabs him, and pushes him away, leading him back to Peppertree. Murk still hasn't said a word and stares at the neighbor upstairs as if Murk was going to take his frustration out on him.

Sheila is walking to Mr. Lee's store and sees Kino with Murk, wearing all Black in a hot-ass hoody sweatshirt. They go back to Peppertree.

"Murk, what the fuck wrong with you? You want to be in prison for the rest of your life?" Kino yells at him.

"I don't give a fuck about prison. Them crackers are going to have to kill me."

"You don't think that I want to kill that nigga too? If we gone, who's gonna take care of mom and look out for your sister? We got to do this right. I don't know how, but some way, somehow, we're going to get that nigga, but we got to do it right," Kino tells Murk.

Murk is mad as hell and knows that Kino's right. But at the same time he's still mad at Kino for stopping him, so he screams letting his frustration out, then charges into Kino full speed and tackles him, as they start wrestling. Bird, Toedoe and Poochy grab Murk to get him off Kino, as they tear up the living room, knocking everything over. Kino doesn't even fight him back; he just tries to get away from Murk's grip while they pry him off of Kino. Toedoe and Murk fly backward and stumble to the ground. Then all of a sudden - "bang!"

Murk's gun went off. Everybody stops moving as they're all in shock. Silence fills the air and they all look at each other, asking if each of them was alright. Everyone responds except Poochy. He fell to the ground, bleeding from his stomach. They all rush to him. Bird holds him in his arms and calls his name as Poochy starts fading in and out of consciousness.

They pick him up and carry him to the car, put him in the back seat as they all get in and rush to the hospital on Mercy Drive. Bird pulls out in front of a car, running it off the road, pushing the pedal to the metal, making them pipes holla. The police see them and take off in pursuit, siren on, now engaged in a high-speed chase. Toedoe tells Bird to put on his flashers as he blows the horn, running people off the road, making it to the hospital in minutes.

He pulls into the emergency room entrance and stops. They get Poochy out of the car and start carrying him inside when the police pull up and draw down on them - "Freeze! Don't move!"

"He's shot! Can't you see?" Kino yells at the officers. The officers look at Poochy and see him fading in and out. Blood is all over him, Bird, Toedoe, Kino and the car. The police put their guns in their holsters.

The nurses and doctors ran out with a bed to get Poochy. The Black woman at the front desk saw them pulling up. She knew something wasn't right from the manner of how they pulled up in a Chevy on 28's. She alerted an emergency, possible gunshot victim needing assistance. They took Poochy right in.

Kino sees the police headed towards them and talks loudly to his click so that everybody can hear him.

"Man, did you see who Poochy was with when we were all in the car getting ready to go to the mall? Then all of a sudden, Poochy came running around the corner saying he was shot." He looks at all of them and then says, "Man, we put him in the car fast as hell and made it here." As the police walk up, he slaps Bird on the shoulder and says, "Good driving bro."

Kino tried to give them the story to tell the police, hoping they would pick up on it and give that same story. They interview Toedoe first.

"I was in the car playing with the CD player and the next thing you know they was putting him in the car, yelling he was shot."

Bird tells them, "I was getting into the car and getting ready to pull off and they said Poochy shot, and before you knew it, they was putting him in the car."

All of them said someone else was putting Poochy in the car, leaving no one left to put him in.

Kino was the last person to be interviewed, and he said that when he came out of his apartment, they were already in the car, so he jumped in before they pulled off.

The officer said, "Well who put him in the car?" Kino thought for a second, as if he was trying to remember. He knew if he said a particular name, there was a chance that person he named might have already said he didn't put him in the car. Instead of Kino trying to think who to say put Poochy in the car, he said, "Maybe he got in on his own, or the people at the apartments helped him to get in the car. All I know is, I heard a gunshot from the side of the building, and I came out to check on my friends, and they said Poochy got shot. When I got to the car he was already in there, so I just hopped in the car with everyone else."

They all said something different, but stated the same event, which is what the police get all the time. So the officers didn't think too much more of it.

You can take five people and have them watch the same event take place, and I guarantee you will get five different stories of that same event. This is what the police go through, even when people are telling their truth.

Kino's story wasn't even the same story he told his compadres to say. They were all in the same ballpark, so hopefully they can make it out of this one.

If Poochy dies, then the investigators will take another turn and try to drill and threaten Kino and his click to tell the truth. If he lives, then it depends on what Poochy tells the police.

- The End –

End Quote

If you learn to take heed of your own and other people's mistakes and failures, and then act upon that knowledge, you will not be in a position wishing you had **One Last Chance.**

-Kaleem 'Abdul 'Adl-

A PREVIEW OF

ONE LAST CHANCE: BOOK TWO
FROM FRIENDS TO ENEMIES

By

KALEEM 'ABDUL 'ADL

CHAPTER ONE

They left the hospital. Bird went to pick up a half of block, get it cooked, and take Kino his eighth. Poochy got out of the hospital and started grinding out of the backyard of his mother's house in Apopka.

Poochy told the detective that some dude was trying to rob him, and he doesn't know who shot him. All he can remember is waking up in the hospital.

Giovani told Dolly and T that Kino didn't set Dolly up and the person Kino brought over to Dolly to buy some dope was a childhood friend of Kino and Murk's.

Murk has been living at the party house, snorting and then going out to rob. Instead of selling dope to snort, he now robs to snort. He'll rob corner stores, gas stations, basers and dope boys, all small- time hustlers.

Bird is now buying a block at a cheaper price. Kino and Poochy get a half, while Bird and Toedoe put in the other half for a whole block.

"After we handle Dolly, the money we make off the next flip, we're going to get Coupe out, right?" Kino asks.

"Derick said them silencers will be here next week," Poochy tells Kino.

They've been staying away from the Palms until they handle Dolly. Kino's been on Polk Street, at The Parliament House, and at Big B's on Ivey Lane. As his clientele grew to niggas buying weight, Kino started to let Murk get all his jugs he had coming to the back of Peppertree. Kino started serving the two brothers Dereck and Pete, and Murk made the back of Peppertree another dope hole on the Drive.

Poochy moves his dope in Taylor's Apartments, on 18th Street, and from the back of his mother's house in Lake Jewel.

Kino and Murk sent Mrs. B. on a vacation back to New Jersey to visit her family for a week. They both gave her a grand a piece.

Bird and Kino are riding to pick up the dope, then Bird is bringing Kino back to Pepper tree.

"Kino, me and Toedoe are ready to split Dolly's wig. They say he be moving a lot of Giovoni's dope out that apartment, bra."

"Patience is everything. Bird, we got to have our money right for lawyers in case something goes wrong," Kino says to Bird.

"We got the choppers, we got the silencers, and we got the money," Bird says.

"I think I want to get him all to myself. It's my fault. I want to take care of my own responsibilities. And killing that nigga is one of my responsibilities," Kino says.

"Shit, you don't think I feel guilty too? It was me who you brought over to him."

"I'ma let you know what's up bro," Kino tells him, then gets his dope and goes into the house. He puts the dope up and flops down on the bed in his room and looks at the ceiling fan spinning thinking about his mother and what happened to her.

Murk walks in and tells Kino, "I can't take it no more bro. I got to kill that nigga with or without you."

Kino pauses and says, "Tonight we going to peel this nigga's wig back."

****

- knocking –

Dolly is looking through the peephole with his .357 in his hand.

"Who dat?"

"It's me, bro."

He lets Giovoni in, then locks the door behind him.

"When you supposed to be moving into your new spot? Renae met with my accountant last month. This is the last

221

time I'm bringing you these blocks to this hole."

"The apartment in Altamonte should be ready next week. They're waiting to put new carpet down," Dolly tells Giovoni

"So you still don't know who did that to Kino's mother?" asks Giovoni.

Dolly lies and says, "Nah bro."

Giovoni looks at him with a smirk face, puts the green duffle bag of bricks down on the table and grabs the duffle bag of money from Dolly, then leaves out.

****

Murk holds up a key and waves it in Kino's face.

"What's that for?" Kino asks.

"It's the key to our success in killing this fuck-nigga."

"What you mean?"

"It's the key to Good Head Jean's house."

"The one who stays across the hall from Dolly?" Kino asks.

"More like a few feet away from Dolly," Murk says with dignity.

"How you get that?"

"Don't worry about that, she left for the weekend and I got the key."

As soon as night hit they loaded up their bags and sneaked into her apartment without being noticed. Inside Good Head Jean's apartment, they moved all of the furniture out of one of the bedrooms, leaving nothing but the walls and the linoleum floor.

They sat on the floor and pulled out the duffle bag, heavy duty trash bags, bleach, rags, two all black outfits, duct-tape, two pistols with silencers, an iron, a lighter, handcuffs, gloves, a spray bottle with water, two bulletproof vests, rope, fake dread wigs, two dark pair of shaded eyeglasses, among other things.

It's ten o'clock at night and Dolly usually goes and chills with Mango for a little while and snort with him in the 9th breezeway, then comes back home.

Kino puts his fake dread wig on and sunglasses, then walks to the 9th breezeway and sees Dolly and Mango hanging outside smoking weed. They don't notice who Kino is, so he heads back to Good Head Jean's apartment.

"He at Mango's house," he tells Murk.

They change their clothes to all Black, put their dread wigs on, the bulletproof vests, then go to the back room that they had cleared out.

The view from that window lets them see when Dolly walks back to his house. The only way Dolly could slip by them from that point of view is if he gets in a car and leaves or comes home the long way around. But if he comes straight back home, they will see him and have at least a one-minute time span before he gets to his door.

They are fully dressed and ready to attack.

"Look, one of us is going to have to lay in the bushes or under the car and see if he goes the other route home. Because if he does, we won't be able to see him when he leaves."

"He's not coming home the long way," Murk says.

"How you know? What if he goes to T's house first before he comes home? Then when he comes home from T's house we'll never see him and he'll be home and we'll be still here looking through this window."

"Oh, I ain't think about that," Murk says.

"If he comes this way text me, and get behind him. I'll see him coming and I'll be waiting for him at his front door. If he goes the other way, follow him and let me know where he's going," Kino tells Murk.

Murk goes and lays in the bushes across the breezeway looking directly at Mango and Dolly.

Kino is sitting in a chair looking out the window, waiting to see Dolly come through that breezeway. His mind goes to wondering as he thinks to himself.

"Is all this hustling worth my mother being molested and pistol-whipped? Is all this dope selling worth me dropping out of school and not going to college? Is all this dope selling worth me quitting my job? Is all this dope selling worth me disappointing and upsetting my mother? Is all this dope selling worth my freedom if I go to jail wishing I had ONE LAST CHANCE? "

Mango and Dolly are about to go inside and pack their noses one last time before Dolly takes it in, when all of a sudden Dolly grabs his .357, squints his eyes, points, and says, "Don't it look like someone's in the bushes over there?"

ABOUT THE AUTHOR

I was born in Philadelphia and raised in Willingboro, New Jersey. I moved to Orlando, Florida when I was in the second grade. I traveled back to New Jersey, spending the summers visiting my friends and relatives who would pick at me because of my Floridian accent. When I went back to Florida as school started, my Floridian friends would then pick at my northern accent. Even though I fluctuated back and forth, I'm a Floridian at heart; a down south rider. Yet all of my family is in Philly, Newark and South Jersey.

I worked at McDonalds at the age of fifteen. I was making $3.35 an hour. Then the crack epidemic hit the Black neighborhoods in Orlando where everyone was broke, poor and struggling. You figure out the rest.

Even though I was raised a Christian and have been baptized, the dirty south bred plenty of racism which propelled me to the Nation of Islam at the age of seventeen, screaming "Fuck them crackers and their religion." I was in and out of jail which was inevitably followed by a prison sentence when I was around twenty years old. This is when Allah Ta'Allah (God the Most High) guided me to true Islam, where I became a Sunni Muslim, erasing racism out of my mind.

Going to prison back in those days in Florida was like a slap on the wrist, with a third of the sentence cut off and CRD. Just as fast as I got out of prison I was just as fast enrolling back into the game, throwing my Islam away.

The streets of Orlando handed me a life of calamities from being car-jacked, robbed and shot, causing me to kill one of the robbers and shooting the other one seven times. This and a whole lot of other things, me and everyone else experienced living in the ghetto.

Eventually, I ventured off into the entertainment field, having a studio designed and built, hosting artists like Rick Ross, Lil Boosie, Gucci Man, Freeway, DJ Khali, Blood Raw and many more to record there. I was also a promoter, bringing concerts and comedy shows to Orlando, Savannah and Washington DC. I brought artists from the likes of Kat Williams and Sheryl Underwood to Lil Wayne, T-Pain, Plies, 8-Ball and M.J.G., to my favorite BGizzal, and a whole host of other celebrities.

After being exhausted trying to make it by spending lots of money in the music industry, I went into filmmaking. I enrolled in college to get a degree in film and video to make a movie. I only had two days left in school to graduate with a degree in film and video when the feds popped me. I was looking at 10 years, but the prosecutor 851'd me, enhancing my sentence to a twenty-year minimum-mandatory sentence, for an old charge I committed 10 years before the instant offense - for a TWENTY DOLLAR rock, because I wouldn't cooperate. In other words, I got TEN EXTRA years for a prior charge, for a twenty-dollar rock, that I already did the time for.   I lost everything except the friends and family who are still riding with me.

Sometimes you have to come down to nothing in order to see who really loves you for YOU and doesn't love you because you're seen as being on top. Because when you're on top, everybody loves you and you can't tell the fake from the real. The best thing I got from this calamity of incarceration is that Allah decreed upon me the correct Islam, the Salafee Manhaj. So I thank Allah for guiding me to the truth and revealing the friends from the foes who were around me.

One Last Chance was the movie I was going to produce after I graduated from college, and I still one day will produce it, inshaa' Allah (God Willing).

Order Your Copy Today
CreateSpace eStore: https://www.createspace.com/6259524

We Help You Self-Publish Your Book

You're The Publisher And We're Your Legs.

We Offer Editing For An Extra Fee, and Highly Suggest It, If Waved, We Print What You Submit!

Crystell Publications is not your publisher, but we will help you self-publish your own novel. **We Offer Editing For An Extra Fee, and Highly Suggest It, If Waived, We Print What You Submit!**

Don't have all your money? .... No Problem!

Ask About our Payment Plans

Crystal Perkins-Stell, MHR
Essence Magazine Bestseller
We Give You Books!
PO BOX 8044 / Edmond – OK 73083
www.crystalstell.com
(405) 414-3991

Don't have all your money up-front.... No Problem!

Ask About our Awesome Pay What You Can Plans

Plan 1-A 190 - 250 pgs $719.00	Plan 1-B 150 -180 pgs $674.00

Plan 1-C 70 - 145pgs $625.00

2 (Publisher/Printer) Proofs, Correspondence, 3 books, Manuscript Scan and Conversion, Typeset, Masters, Custom Cover, ISBN, Promo in Mink, 2 issues of Mink Magazine, Consultation, POD uploads. 1 Week of E-blast to a reading population of over 5000 readers, book clubs, and bookstores, The Authors Guide to Understanding The POD, and writing Tips, and a review snippet along with a professional query letter will be sent to our top 4 distributors in an attempt to have your book shelved in their bookstores or distributed to potential book vendors. After the query is sent, if interested in your book, distributors will contact you or your outside rep to discuss shipment of books, and fees.

Plan 2-A 190 - 250 pgs $645.00	Plan 2-B 150 -180 pgs $600.00

Plan 2-C 70 - 145pgs $550.00

1 Printer Proof, Correspondence, 3 books, Manuscript Scan and Conversion, Typeset, Masters, Custom Cover, ISBN, Promo in Mink, 1 issue of Mink Magazine, Consultation, POD upload.

We're Changing The Game.

No more paying Vanity Presses $8 to $10 per book! We Give You Books @ Cost.

Made in the USA
Middletown, DE
28 October 2022